ff

JOSEPHINE

Kenneth Lillington

faber and faber

LONDON · BOSTON

First published in 1989
by Faber and Faber Limited
3 Queen Square London WC1N 3AU

Photoset by Parker Typesetting Service Leicester
Printed in Great Britain by
Richard Clay Ltd Bungay Suffolk

© Kenneth Lillington, 1989

British Library Cataloguing in Publication Data is available

ISBN 0-571-15379-8

For Phyllis Hunt

CHAPTER ONE

One afternoon in the autumn of 1932, the year in which the Yo-Yo craze was sweeping England, Mr Johnson, Housemaster, was sitting at his desk reading a letter, when Porson, the House Captain, came in.

'Weekly House report, sir.'

'Yes, Porson. All serene?'

'Yes, sir. Except that Bannington Major has broken his arm and Forbes-Ponsonby has concussion, sir. Actually we thought he was dead but he's come round now, only he still groans a bit, sir.'

'Rugger practice?'

'No, in detention, sir,'

'So what were they up to in detention?'

'Acting the giddy goat, sir.'

'Who was the duty master, Porson?'

'Mr Cropper, sir.'

'Oh.'

'Yes, sir.'

'Oh, well,' said Mr Johnson, with a sigh, 'tell me what happened.'

'Well, sir, everyone started chucking paper darts about, sir, and Pontifex got out a mouth organ and started playing it, sir, and then Mr Cropper jumped up on the table and shouted, "You common cry of curs, whose breath I hate as reek o' the rotten fens, whose loves I prize as the dead carcasses of unburied men who do corrupt my air, I banish you," sir. Then he got the double-headed axe from the museum cupboard and swiped Bannington Major on the arm and cracked Forbes-Ponsonby on the head, sir.'

'Was there any panic?'

'No, sir, because Fearless of the Fifth showed presence of mind, sir, and switched out the lights, and the class managed to make a bolt for it, sir.'

'Unusual for Fearless to be in detention.'

'Yes, sir. Actually, it's generally believed that he was covering up for Cardew, sir.'

'That's strange company for Fearless.'

'It may be that he's trying to convert him into a jolly decent chap, sir.'

'So Fearless switched out the lights. What did Mr Cropper do then?'

'He fell down frothing at the mouth, sir.'

'I'm afraid Mr Cropper lives in a world of his own, Porson.'

'Yes, sir.'

'Well, now: here's another matter – '

But at this point Porson spotted Mr Cropper through the window, and Mr Johnson followed his gaze. Mr Cropper was ambling across the Quad like a pre-occupied sheep. He was of straggly build, as if he had been thrown together in a hurry. He had a small round face of exceeding innocence, with straw-coloured hair.

'Perhaps, after that outburst, he's settled down for a bit,' said Mr Johnson.

'The Lower Corridor's still a risk, sir. He turns into a Cavalier in the Lower Corridor.'

'You know the old school pretty well, don't you, Porson?'

'Have to, to survive, sir.'

'To be sure. Now, Porson: I want to ask you a straight question. What's the House's attitude to girls?'

'*Girls*, sir?'

'Let's be frank, Porson. Girls.'

'Well . . . some fellows have sisters, sir.'

'True,' said Mr Johnson, and appeared struck by this. 'True.'

Porson hesitated. 'I don't think fellows think all that much about . . . *Them*, sir. They've got compulsory games, sir.'

'How would they react if one appeared in their midst?'

'Probably be annoyed, sir. It's difficult to punt a ball about with some girl getting in the way.'

'Then prepare to be annoyed. One is coming here.'

'*Here*, sir?'

'Yes, and we can't refuse. She's the Headmaster's niece.'

Porson's face cleared. 'Oh, you mean she's coming on Speech Day, sir? Oh, that's all right, sir. We'll make sure that Cardew gets put in detention – '

'No, she's coming here as a pupil. Eagles House. In the Sixth. For a term.'

'Lord,' said Porson faintly.

'Her school has had to close because of an epidemic of measles and the Head's letting her carry on here. Her – er – safe conduct will be your responsibility.'

'I can't keep Cardew in detention for a whole term, sir,' said Porson glumly.

'Oh, don't anticipate trouble. Girls do exist, and there's no blinking the fact. This girl may well be some fellow's sister. So why should there be any silly excitement?'

'What's she like, sir?' asked Porson guardedly.

'I've never met her, but her name's J. Tugnutt and she's the Head's niece.'

'I see what you mean, sir,' said Porson, brightening.

'Quite. Doesn't sound like a *femme fatale*, does she?'

'Oh, I say. No, she doesn't, sir. Actually, sir, this could do the House some good. I mean, disillusion them, lower their temperature a bit. So long as the girl is awful enough, sir.'

'Steady, Porson. The Head's niece, you know. But I take your point.'

There was a timid knock at the door. Porson opened it to admit Trubbs Minor of the Second.

'Please, sir,' began Trubbs, his eyes bulging behind his thick glasses.

'Am I invisible, you little snipe?' said Porson.

'Oh! No, Porson. Sorry, Porson. Please, Porson –'

'Are you aware that you're in the presence of your Housemaster, you little worm?'

'Oh! Sorry, Porson. Please, sir –'

'Do you suppose the Housemaster wants to listen to your babbling, you little freak?'

'No, Porson. Sorry, Porson. Please, Porson –'

'Have you anything to say, you little moron?'

'Yes, Porson. Please, Porson.'

'Then out with it, you little cretin.'

By now Trubbs's tie had worked round under one ear, the point of his collar had got into his mouth, he was the colour of beetroot, panting heavily and streaming with perspiration. He managed to stammer, 'Please, Porson, please, sir, there's a girl to see you.'

'Well, really,' said Mr Johnson mildly, 'it took a long time to tell me that simple fact, didn't it? Show her in, Trubbs, and stop being a little ass.'

Trubbs gulped and swallowed. 'Please, sir, I can't, sir. She's in the Quad, sir. Surrounded by a colossal crowd, sir. Practically the whole school, sir.'

Porson went to the window.

4

'Gosh,' he said in a hushed voice.

'Well?' said Mr Johnson.

'I can 't see . . . *her* all that well, sir. She keeps being hidden by the crowd. She's – she's not quite what we expected, sir.'

Mr Johnson joined him at the window. J. Tugnutt, below, had come into view.

'Would that be . . . sort of . . . a *femme fatale*, sir?' asked Porson anxiously.

'Let's hope she's not actually fatal,' said Mr Johnson, 'but I'm afraid a lot of fellows may be on the danger list.'

Josephine Tugnutt was excusably nervous as she walked up the tree-lined avenue that led to St Chauvin's College. One girl among six hundred boys! She came from a girls' boarding school, and was walking into the unknown.

At last she reached the Quad, emerging from the trees with a copper sun glowing behind her. And thus, an English rose aureoled in autumn light, was she beheld by Trubbs Minor, who had bandaged his hand to get out of rugger practice and was slinking away to smoke a cigarette behind the rhododendrons. She had the same effect on him as the goddess Athena, dropping from a cloud, would have had on a susceptible Ancient Greek.

'Girl!' he exclaimed in a shrill squeak.

Josephine hailed him with relief. 'Excuse me, could you tell me where to find Mr Johnson? I'm the new Sixth Form pupil.'

'Gosh!'

'Do you think you could possibly – '

'Oh yes. Gosh, yes,' said Trubbs. He turned scarlet and the point of his collar got stuck in his mouth. 'The Beak. Yes.'

'Thank you.' But Josephine now took stock of Trubbs, who was quivering like a ribbon on a fan. 'But are you feeling all right? You're shivering, and you've hurt your hand. Perhaps you should see a doctor.'

'Oh no, really. I say, what name shall I say?'

'Josephine Tugnutt.'

'Gosh.'

As they stepped into the open quadrangle, it filled with boys in rugger kit. The word 'girl' had caused this. Even in class, come across in print, it would send a shiver through them. Squeaked by Trubbs Minor, and supported by the sight of a real live one with the sun behind her, it drew them like prospectors to a gold rush, or rats to where there is garbage.

The boys surrounded Josephine in silence and amazement. She felt like a street accident.

The situation was saved by a handsome boy who approached with lounging grace and said agreeably, 'Did I hear you say you wanted Mr Johnson? I'll take you to him.'

'Thank you,' said Josephine gratefully. Trubbs Minor had scudded frantically away and had disappeared round a corner of the nearest building. The crowd of stunned onlookers made way for them.

'Charming weather for the time of year,' remarked the handsome youth.

'Yes, it is.'

'This Yo-Yo craze seems to be sweeping the country.'

'Yes, it does.'

'May I introduce myself? Fearless of the Fifth.'

'Josephine Tugnutt. I think I'm to be Of the Sixth.'

'You're one up on me, then,' said Fearless, with what Josephine, who had read some school stories, recognized as a cheery grin. He really was most pleasant, and never at a loss, and perfect at putting her at her ease.

They came to an iron staircase. 'Mr Johnson's room is up there,' said Fearless, pointing to a window only a few feet up. Mr Johnson was looking out of it but hastily drew back when Josephine saw him. Fearless then led her further along the path that led away from it.

'Shouldn't we go up those stairs, then?'

'No, only Sixth Formers are allowed to use the iron staircase.'

'How ridiculous.' She immediately regretted saying this, but Fearless smiled.

'Quite ridiculous. Between ourselves, the place could do with shaking up. Tradition, you know.'

'Are there a lot of traditions?'

'Any number.'

They made a wide detour, finally entering the Masters' Corridor from the other side of the building. A tall, aloof-looking boy of about eighteen came out of Mr Johnson's room.

'Tugnutt?'

'Yes.'

'Yes, Porson.'

'Oh. Yes, Porson.'

'Come in, Tugnutt.'

He made way for her, and remained standing by the door like a sentry. Mr Johnson, in contrast, strove to be light and casual and made a most uncomfortable job of it. He ejaculated, 'Jolly good!' at intervals, and laughed in the manner of a vicar. He kept putting his pipe in his mouth and removing it and waving it about. Not once did he look her in the eyes, glancing at the coal-scuttle, the ceiling and his own feet. Josephine stood with her hands modestly clasped in front of her and lowered her gaze, wondering meanwhile whether the pair of them, if unscrewed at the neck, would turn out to be operated by clockwork. Porson would be a toy soldier and this

7

housemaster person a manikin in a shop window, advertising tobacco perhaps, continually bringing its pipe to its mouth in a series of jerks.

When the interview was over Porson said, 'Your room is in Matron's quarters,' and led the way, briskly, so that she had to hurry after him with her valise. Occasionally he glanced round. She almost expected him to say, 'Heel!'

The Matron had an apartment in a distant block of buildings on the boundary of the school grounds. Porson halted at the entrance and looked at her dispassionately.

'You'll be all right here,' he said distantly, 'so long as you Fit In.'

'I'll try,' said Josephine. She felt as if she had stepped on to an alien planet. ' – Porson,' she added.

CHAPTER TWO

Having been introduced to the Matron, and made sure that her luggage had arrived, Josephine was taken to see her uncle, the Headmaster. He visited her home rarely but her father's surgery frequently, his hobby being hypochondria. His generosity in letting Josephine join his school was really an investment. A doctor who felt morally obliged to overlook his fees was worth cultivating.

He was a man who, ever since his boyhood, had eagerly awaited the time when his body would catch up with the middle-age spread in his mind and had now triumphed, having a bald head, a booming voice, a bulging paunch and a hernia. He looked at the ceiling and boomed over her head.

'And how is your father?'

'He is very well, thank you, Uncle.'

'And your brothers?'

'Very well, thank you, Uncle. They're both studying medicine.'

'Ah yes. I wish them every success.'

Josephine was encouraged to volunteer, 'I want to study medicine, too.'

'Ah, to you, my dear, I wish Happiness.'

By which he meant, thought Josephine, the exquisite happiness of staying at home and darning someone's

9

socks. She made up her mind that when she left school she would be as unhappy as possible.

She had dreaded meeting Matron, whom she had expected to be like a wardress in a nineteenth-century jail, but she was a pleasant surprise: a motherly woman with a kind, slightly weary smile.

'I *am* glad to have you here, Josephine. It'll be someone to talk to.'

To be called Josephine again all but brought tears to her eyes. They sat by the fire and ate buttered toast and chatted agreeably. Josephine described her father and brothers, and her old school, and the subjects she was to study in the Sixth.

'Chemistry, biology and physics,' remarked Matron. 'What job do you want to do?'

'I'd like to be a doctor, and after I've qualified I'd like to specialize in psychiatry.'

'*Really?* Well, good luck to you, Josephine. We need psychiatrists, Heaven knows.'

Psychiatry, in 1932, was almost as much of a cult as the Yo-Yo, but for all that it seemed to Josephine that Matron spoke with some personal heat. Whom did she mean by 'we'? 'I'?

Josephine saw very little of the boys in general. She spent her private study periods in Matron's room, and she ate her meals there too. The Science Sixth had few members, and in the biology class, taught by a dark genius named Mr Victor, she happened to be the only pupil. And yet, in the few days that followed her arrival, the morale of Eagles House plummeted to the abyss. The First Fifteen lost 57–0 to Badgers, and the rotten little swot Hopkins of the Fourth was caught writing a poem. Seven boys, off their guard, were injured by Mr Cropper, and Fanshawe-Smith of the

Classical Sixth joined a monastery, leaving behind a desperate note with a postscript that if his mater sent him any tuck it was to be forwarded to Woebegone Abbey for Brother Bartholomew, which was his monkish name.

It used to be said that a woman on board ship brought bad luck to the crew. Perhaps a girl aboard St Chauvin's did likewise, but Josephine could not see where she had gone wrong. She had done her best to Fit In. Deeming a gym-slip unsuitable in male company, she wore dark, high-waisted, pleated skirts of mid-calf length (the immodest short skirts of the 1920's had gone out of fashion) and formal white blouses. She assumed a demure demeanour and sometimes wore big round horn-rimmed spectacles, but her effect was everywhere the same, and what was more, she got no satisfaction from it. In her chemistry and physics classes she might have been watching something on the stage for all the notice that the boys and masters took of her, and yet her presence was like a time-bomb ticking away. If this was what it was like to be a *femme fatale*, she'd rather play hockey.

In her attempt to Fit In, she watched the Eagles–Badgers match flanked by Fearless of the Fifth and Porson, who had put a reserve in the team in order to stand guard over her. Fearless, Josephine noticed, did not seem to play much himself but he gave his side excellent advice, calling out, 'Heel it out *nicely*, Eagles!' like an officer commanding his troops. Porson was silent and even sulky. How badly he showed up beside Fearless!

It takes two sides to make a game, and Eagles played with such depressing apathy that Badgers occasionally gave up scoring and the ball lay on the ground ignored. Feeling vaguely guilty, Josephine strove to urge her side on. In the manner of Fearless, she called out, 'Heel it out *naice*leigh, Eagles!' with all her might, but her girl's voice sounded weak and out of place and the only effect it had was to make the Eagles team turn and stare at her.

She realized that some of the rumours she had heard about the school customs were false. New boys were not pinned by their ears to the door of the Fives Court, nor were Second Form boys made to drag Sixth Formers about in rickshaws. She was, however, shocked at the Sixth Formers' way of addressing their juniors. She said so to Fearless of the Fifth.

'I don't think they should call those little boys snipes, worms, freaks, morons and cretins.'

'But they're sprogs,' said Fearless good-naturedly. 'Sprogs' was the St Chauvin's word for juniors.

'Well, I think it's rude.'

'Yes, perhaps it is,' said Fearless with disarming candour. 'Perhaps we could do with more feminine influence in this school. It might do us all a world of good.'

He was a delightful fellow. She thought it a pity that he went about so much with Cardew of the Remove, an obvious cad who, whenever he saw Josephine, directed at her a leer so significant that it was almost an assault, but the tolerant Fearless seemed to see good in everyone.

She wished she could speak to him more often but to her annoyance Porson kept turning up, like a policeman on his beat.

'I'm afraid I'm being a nuisance to you,' she said pointedly.

'That's all right.'

'Please don't give yourself so much trouble.'

'That's all right.'

Once, as he followed Josephine along a corridor, he

suddenly pushed her into a broom cupboard. She was surprised and even displeased but she didn't protest, supposing that this must be another of St Chauvin's traditions. All Porson said was, 'Cropper in the offing.'

Once, unexpectedly, he asked her, 'Do you like Fearless?'

'Yes, I do. Shouldn't I?'

'Of course. He's a jolly decent chap,' said Porson stiffly.

But why stiffly? She disliked him even more.

A little later Porson told Mr Johnson, 'I wish to resign the House Captaincy, sir.'

Mr Johnson glanced at him with a twinge of misgiving. Sometimes (though he felt a traitor for doing so) he doubted whether Porson was ideally suited to be a House Captain. He was not self-assured enough. He too often looked worried. If Mr Johnson hadn't known him so well, he might have suspected him of introspection. Not altogether healthy.

'Why, Porson?'

'I can no longer handle the job, sir. It's . . . ' Porson seemed for a few moments to be strangling himself, 'it's Tugnutt, sir. It's just that she's *there*, sir.'

'But whom do you suggest that I appoint in your place? Trubbs Minor?'

'There's Fearless of the Fifth, sir.'

'Yes,' said Mr Johnson thoughtfully, 'he has a reputation for utter decency.'

'Yes, sir, and he's got initiative. Like yesterday in Assembly, sir. When – ' Porson gulped and drew a breath – 'when *she* arrived the whole school turned round to look at her as if they were hypnotized, sir. Just before the masters came in. And Fearless borrowed Pontifex's mouth organ and played "God Save the

King'', sir. Which brought them to their feet, sir.'

'Well, I'll keep Fearless as First Reserve, but hang on a bit longer, Porson, there's a good chap.'

'Very good, sir,' said Porson resignedly, and left the room. He stood outside the door for a moment, his face like that of a Red Indian at the stake who lets just a hint of his suffering show through his fortitude.

Josephine herself, who of course had been most embarrassed by the mouth organ incident, had been particularly struck with the look that Fearless had given her just after it. It had been – what was the word? – *speculative*. Rather odd. But there, he was a good chap and splendid in a crisis.

Porson's words, 'Cropper in the offing', seemed to Josephine to be needlessly alarming. Mr Cropper looked a frail old man who would collapse like a deck-chair at a mere push. Why did everyone scatter at his approach? Perhaps dodging the English master was yet another of St Chauvin's traditions?

Seeing him once at the end of a long corridor, when Porson was in class and unable to tail her, she did feel a little nervous, but she held her head high and marched forward. All Mr Cropper did was to halt in front of her, study her gravely, bow deeply, and with the words, 'Madam, my card,' hand her a picture card from a packet of cigarettes.

'Yes, he has such beautiful manners,' said her friend the Matron, when Josephine told her of this.

'But why should he give me a picture of – ', Josephine examined the card, – 'Stephenson's Rocket, 1815?'

'Poor gentleman, he lives in a world of his own.'

'Don't they all!'

'Don't be too sorry for him, Josephine!' And Matron told her of some of Mr Cropper's ravages. Josephine was sorrier for him than for his victims. Matron perceived this, and liked her all the more. Indeed, she was on the brink of taking Josephine into her confidence over some matter of her own. Josephine sensed this, and was naturally curious; but Matron let it pass. Instead she said, 'Ah well, he's lucky to be working in a public school. Anywhere else, and they'd have put him in a home long ago.'

'He'd be far better off in one,' said Josephine.

What Matron did not know was how Mr Cropper had come to get into his own world, and it should be explained how this had come about.

Nineteen thirty-two was a slump year, with nigh on three million unemployed, so Mr Cropper was lucky to have a job at all; but lucky to work at St Chauvin's? The life of the teacher who is unsuited to teaching is not a happy one. Mr Cropper's pupils put drawing pins in his chair, fixed the pegs of the blackboard so that it guillotined his feet, chopped bits off his gown with specially imported scissors and threw ink on his trousers. In his desk they put toads and live rats and, on one occasion, a dreadful jack-in-the-box with a death's head, which sprang to the height of three feet at him with a noise like an orchestra of Jew's harps.

A sensitive man, Mr Cropper was of course much affected by all this, but his final state, in which he mixed up fact and fiction and fantasy, was caused by one of those bizarre coincidences which, guard ourselves as we will, so often make or mar our lives. He taught, or rather failed to teach, English literature, and was a studious reader of tedious books on that subject. One day he went to the public library in the town. The librarian on duty was a wretched girl who had recently become infatuated with a pimply boy of no account. She was day-dreaming about him when Mr Cropper appeared, asking for a book on the Romantic Movement. Her mind besotted with the thought of romance, she looked at him with glazed eyes and then, instead of directing him to the card index, she pointed vaguely towards the section for Light Romances, where the historical romances of Elise Bobbin throbbed on the shelves.

Mr Cropper peered along the rows of these, all soberly alike in their green library bindings. Doubtfully, he picked one out. It was entitled *Girl Wife: A Drama of Regency Days*. Leaning against the shelves, he began reading.

The story was about Lady Euphemia, nineteen, green-eyed, lovely and unsophisticated, who became the bride of devil-may-care, fabulously rich Lord Ravensbourne as a result of a crazy wager that he would marry the very next girl he set eyes on. The news of this wager got round and a queue of girls formed outside Ravensbourne Towers, with buskers and hot-dog stalls in attendance. Euphemia climbed in through the window of the Gents where Lord Ravensbourne was hiding, and became the first lovely, unsophisticated girl to set foot there. He admitted the challenge, with that sardonic twist to his eyebrows that made him irresistible to women, and they were married at once by his personal chaplain, after which they ascended to a balcony where they amused themselves watching his lordship's flunkeys setting the dogs on the other girls.

Elise Bobbin had introduced Mr Cropper to escapist literature, and he, under the thin skin of his education, had a need for escapism such as the diabetic has for insulin. He was enthralled. Slowly he slid down the shelves until he was sitting on the floor, his legs stuck out, still reading. Other borrowers tripped over his feet. Without moving from the spot, he read the novel right through.

From then on he was addicted to Elise Bobbin's writings. He found her books, in their lurid covers, on every bookstall, and those of other writers like her: Deborah Cartilege, Elsie M. Dingle. He was, of course, an intellectual snob and hid them under his coat like stolen goods, but the notion that they were forbidden fruit increased the intensity of their effect on him. He secreted them in his room and devoured them by the dozen. Gradually they replaced what the world in general would call reality. One day he found a fencer's épée from somewhere, strode out on to the rugger field and with a cry of, 'Ha, ye dogs, so ye have the guts to play, ecod?' inflicted grievous gashes on three members of the Second Fifteen.

The parents of the three boys were awfully decent about it and the matter was quietly dropped, but Mr Cropper had tasted blood and from then on, like Genghis Khan, he left a devastation behind him. This did not deter his pupils in their unruly behaviour. Rather, it gave them a zest for daring, and it became a mark of honour with the boys of Eagles House to bear scars or exhibit a mutilation.

CHAPTER THREE

'Matron,' asked Josephine, 'why doesn't anyone take biology in the Sixth?'

'They've all given it up.'

'You mean Mr Victor teaches only the little boys?'

'He used to. Not now.'

'Doesn't he teach anyone?'

'Not now. Only you. The Headmaster has arranged the timetable so that no one takes biology any more. There was some trouble a while back, when Mr Victor started using some of the boys for human experiments. Oh, I don't think he wanted to *dissect* them or anything like that, you know, but unfortunately it happened just before Open Day, and when the parents came, some of the junior boys were clucking like chickens, and there was a scaremonger rumour that one of them had turned into a wolf. I dare say the whole thing was exaggerated, but some of the parents made a fuss and said surely this is not what we're paying those high fees for. So Mr Victor's classes were taken away from him. Of course it gives him more time for his research, but I think he gets lonely, poor man.'

Mr Victor made no attempt to ease his loneliness with discourse. He gave Josephine a set of notes, dog-eared from years of handling, and retreated to a high lab stool on which he sat hunched over like Rodin's 'Thinker'.

Josephine knew no men, apart from her busy father and her hearty, good-natured brothers, who treated her as a jolly kid, but she had read about them in books and Mr Victor was the very picture of what she had read about mad scientists. He was tall and haggard, with a lock of dark hair across his brow and deep-set burning eyes.

For several lessons he seemed not to notice her existence but she knew that it was making itself felt, as it did everywhere here, and tension built up like the atmosphere before a storm. One morning he began pacing about, occasionally throwing himself theatrically into chairs and brooding. From such an attitude he eventually spoke in a staccato voice.

'How long did it take God to make the world?'

'Seven days, I think.'

'No, no, no. Millions of years.'

'Ah yes, evolution.'

'Evolution. Millions of years of bungling experiment. Look at all the creatures He made to reach Man. Obscenities like head-lice. Absurdities like the three-toed sloth. Millions of years of trial and error to reach Man – who is still mostly error. It has taken me – if you omit preliminary research – *six weeks*. I admit that God did the pioneer work and left me the ingredients. But I'm the logical successor – the next dialectic step forward. Or you might say, God is taller than I but I stand on God's shoulders.'

Josephine kept an eye on the door. 'I don't understand, sir.'

'Of course you don't.'

Hoping that the conversation was over Josephine turned back to her notes, but in a few moments Mr Victor came up and gripped the edge of her desk with his bony hands. Looking up apprehensively, she

19

found herself gazing into his eyes, within which moved strange lights.

'I believe', he said, in low and vibrant tones, 'that I have discovered the ray that brought life into the world.'

'Congratulations,' said Josephine doubtfully.

She was rather alarmed. Mr Victor's claim to be superior to God seemed excessive and it was likely that he was simply off his head, perhaps from having been dropped on it in infancy or perhaps from the effect that St Chauvin's seemed to have, in differing ways, on everyone; but there was a compulsive quality about him that deterred one from dismissing him out of hand.

She tried politely to put him off. 'It's too advanced for me, sir,' she said. 'I haven't got Higher Schools yet, and this must be post-degree work.'

Mr Victor burst startlingly into derisive laughter. 'Ha-ha-ha-ha-ha! Post degree! Do you think any footling little MSc or PhD could understand it? I am as superior to them as the common man is to the chimpanzee.'

'Miles beyond me, then.' But Mr Victor was in a state of exultation and was not listening. He pointed to a door at the end of the lab.

'You cannot guess what lies beyond there.'

Josephine looked fearfully at the unimpressive door. What did lie behind it? Perhaps a necromancer's den, an agglomeration of hocus-pocus medieval and modern: articles of witchcraft, including skulls and pictures of baleful goats, side by side with bits of mystery apparatus consisting of dials, screens and flashing bulbs, and in the centre an operating table supporting a grisly figure . . .

Mr Victor's claims were not modest but she was not in a position to reject them. He was an adult, she an adolescent; he was a teacher, she a student. Besides, however wild a claim may be, we always have a niggling doubt about it. We've been wrong so often. They all laughed at Christopher Columbus, Galileo, Edison, Marconi, the Wright brothers . . .

Mr Victor became low and vibrant again.

'I am on the brink of creating a Man.'

The grisly figure on the table now took shape in Josephine's mind. It would be put together from corpses dug from graves, with stitches all over it and nuts and bolts through its neck. Its huge hands would dangle from wrists sticking out from sleeves too short for it. Mr Victor having carelessly supplied it with the brain of a hanged criminal, it would go about strangling people. It would be superhumanly strong and quite unkillable, rising again and again from swamps and the ashes of fires . . .

Nervousness made her foolish. 'A man?' she said. 'Aren't there rather a lot of them about already?'

'But don't you see what this means?' said Mr Victor urgently. 'He will have been made, not born. He will be the first truly Existential Man. He will be really, truly, utterly alone. No past life, no race, no kith and kin, no God, no sex — '

'Not much fun, either,' remarked Josephine.

'He will be Free. Totally, absolutely Free.'

'I wish him luck,' said Josephine. 'When will he be born?'

'The Ray will decide that.'

'Oh yes,' said Matron, in her placid, reassuring way, 'Mr Victor does have some strange fancies. He is too much alone, poor man.'

'I'm not altogether surprised.'

'He's too brilliant for ordinary society. They say he's wonderfully clever.'

21

Mad genius, after all? Would it be wrong to write him off too quickly?

'It's a pity he can't take classes as he used to,' said Matron. 'They would be company for him. That Open Day Business was so unfortunate. It's possible that those boys were only pretending to cluck like chickens. Little boys can be naughty.'

'I suppose they started the rumour about the wolf, too?'

'Well, the trouble was that a wolf actually *was* seen in the Quad – '

'What? A real live one?'

'Yes. I expect it had escaped from a circus.'

'They don't have wolves in circuses,' protested Josephine. 'They have lions and tigers and elephants, but not wolves.'

'Well, then, perhaps from a zoo.'

'There are no zoos within miles of here!'

'But can't wolves run a long way?' asked Matron vaguely. 'Fifty miles a day, I've heard.'

'What did they do to the wolf?' Josephine turned pale. 'They didn't shoot it, did they?'

'No, it escaped. They've never caught it. Haven't you heard of the Dorset Wolf?'

'Good gracious! Yes I have!' She remembered now: it cropped up from time to time in the papers, a shadowy grey form spotted by hikers in the Dorset woods or sometimes caught in the headlights of cars in bylanes. It had been explained away as a stray Alsatian dog, or a mere figment of the imagination.

But not by everyone. Some people swore to having seen it and would not be gainsaid.

Laughing at explorers, discoverers and pioneers was all too common . . .

Perhaps there was something to Mr Victor's wild notions after all?

Matron was smiling at her with great affection.

'Don't look so worried, Jo.' (She now called Josephine Jo.) 'Gentlemen have their funny ideas, you know. You take them too seriously.'

CHAPTER FOUR

Whenever Trubbs Minor's fellow sprogs came near him, they kicked him, on the grounds that he was a Weed. This was his only contact with them.

After he had met Josephine he had enjoyed a brief popularity. The Second Formers gathered round him in the dorm to hear how he had met This Girl coming into the Quad. They scorned girls officially, but wondered at them in secret, and there was not one of them who had not been stunned by Josephine's personal appearance. Having seen the great Fearless himself treat her as an equal, they saw fit to accord Trubbs some respect and even envy. But it did not last. Trubbs was not up to taking advantage even of this piece of fortune.

'What were you doing in the Quad, anyway, when you ought to have been playing rugger, you toad?'

'The fact is, you fellows, the Beak told me to go and meet her –'

Howls of derision, accompanied by kicks.

'The Beak told *you*?'

'Did he want her to think she'd come to a zoo, you freak?'

'You know what, you men? Trubbs was skiving off to smoke a fag in the bushes!'

'He'd bandaged his hand up, the slacker!'

'Let's rag the smoky rotter, chaps!'

Trubbs hated being a Weed. He would have scored innumerable tries, made centuries, knocked out the best fighter in the form and been chaired shoulder high by his cheering schoolfellows; only it was his glasses, you see. Nor did he get on better with his teachers who beat him almost daily, ostensibly for his academic shortcomings but basically for being a Weed. He had long decided that he was No Good.

This he had kept to himself till now. When he wrote to his parents, who had all but bankrupted themselves to send their two sons to this expensive school, he always began in the same way: 'Dear Mater and Pater, I am having a topping time . . .'

When he had met Josephine it seemed to him that his luck at last had turned round, but it was not to be. A Weed was his lifestyle. He was No Good.

He decided to run away.

To sea? You heard of fellows running away to sea. Weymouth was not far away. Perhaps some captain would take him on as a cabin boy. He would have to rough it, of course. Perhaps they'd keel-haul him. It couldn't be worse than St Chauvin's.

All day, by stages, he packed a small attaché case, not forgetting to put in a bar of chocolate and a packet of cigarettes, and deep into the night when his fellow pupils, tired out from having bumped him and tossed him in a blanket, were fast asleep, he dressed himself under cover of the bedclothes, and carrying his shoes, his attaché case and his top hat, crept out into the corridor, down the stairs, and out into the Quad.

He edged his way round the walls and came to the path that led through the wood to the main gate. Walking on the grass verge to soften his steps, he set out on his trek from the school.

The worst was over. He would climb over the main

gate and run, run, run into the night.

Moonlight bathed the trees and threw their sharp black shadows across the path. The walk was much longer than he had reckoned. The woods were ghostly. He heard a noise, distinct from the woodland rustlings. It was his own breathing. Wasn't it? To reassure himself he stopped and held his breath. The breathing continued, heavier now, like sawing wood.

It was accompanied by the patter of feet.

He hurried on, walking so fast that he pained his legs. He *would* run away! He broke into a run, gasping so loud that he could hear no other sound.

A grey form slipped from the shadows and barred his way. He saw the grin of the fangs, the wicked glitter in the shallow yellow eyes.

He backed away, dripping with perspiration, his teeth chattering.

'Look, old chap, I'm on your side. Always thought it jolly rotten of old Victor to do this to you. Not that you're not all right, of course, old chap. But if there's anything I can do, old chap.'

But he lacked all conviction. Protestations, pleading, attempts to be friendly succeeded only in making his schoolfellows nastier to him than ever and there was no reason to suppose that becoming a wolf would have softened this one up. He backed farther away. The Dorset Wolf did not move. It had never been a sociable wolf, and no one had caught more than a glimpse of it, which was why so many people declared that it was only a shadow, a trick of the light. Perhaps Trubbs was seeing things, but nothing on earth would induce him to put it to the test. Suddenly he turned, and, holding his hat on, bolted back towards the Quad, expecting fangs in his rear at every step.

He doubled up by the wall, an asthmatic attack upon

him so that his breathing sounded like a broken concertina. Someone would hear him, surely, and he would be caught and beaten with extra severity to convince him of the merits of remaining at the school. But no one came, and his frantic gasps subsided to a dry sobbing. Creep back, then, and sneak into bed? He would sooner die than do that. And so he dared go neither back nor forward, but stayed crouching in the shadows.

It then occurred to him that there was another way out.

The building that contained Matron's quarters was on the very edge of the grounds. The walls were covered with ancient ivy and at one corner there was a row of garages, only about eight feet high. He could climb on to the roofs of these and somehow, by drainpipes or some other fearful foothold, scramble into the field beyond. Trubbs was as frightened of heights as he was of all the other hazards of this life but his cause was desperate. Once more, then, the furtive circumnavigation of the wall, past the door to his own block, on to the archway under the clock in the main building and along the bleak stone corridor that led through to the Lower Quad. To be in this corridor was terrifying, because it led into the very heart of the school and, try as he might, he could not subdue the noise of his breathing. But the school slumbered on and he emerged into the Lower Quad, and went once more through the routine of sidling round the walls.

At last he reached the garages. No ivy covered their doors, of course. He would have to climb up by the building at their side. Gosh, a window was open right in front of him! He would have to pass it on his way up! The thought of the climb sickened him, but the thought of going back was worse. He reached out and grasped a stem of ivy. It came away in his hand. He tried again,

27

found a stem that held this time, bent a knee, stuck a foot into the leafy mass, hauled, straightened, and hung there on one hand and one foot.

It is not easy to climb an ivy-clad wall when you are wearing a top hat and carrying an attaché case. Trubbs, two feet above the ground, looked up. The garages had acquired an appalling height. He *must* do it! The window sill was on a level with his free left foot. If he planted that foot on it for a second . . .

A terrible paroxysm of coughing seized him. His strength had all run out and he knew that to climb to the roof was impossible. He keeled over, utterly defeated, intent now solely on dropping back to the ground. His top hat fell off his head, hit the window sill, and bounced inside the room.

In consternation he slid down, put down his case, and with a last effort heaved himself over the sill and half into the room. He groped for his hat. The backs of his fingers touched it. It rolled farther away into the room.

This had the effect of the final blow given to a stricken boxer on the ropes. Trubbs hung over the window sill like a rag doll. Josephine, in bed in that room, was awakened by a sound like inexpert bagpipe practice.

Her first thought was that some St Chauvin's ritual must be taking place. She was not yet adjusted to the madness of this school. Her own boarding school had been mad, of course, but it had been a ladylike madness, a madness of dainty stitches making up a network of finicky rules and fatuous prohibitions. The madness here was of a coarser grain: male.

She switched on her bedside lamp, decided very quickly that Trubbs Minor was draped over her sill through mishap rather than intention, switched the light off, put on a dressing gown, and lugged him into the room.

'C-c-case,' he panted, flapping a hand at the window. 'C-c-case.'

'Sh-sh.'

She went through the open window with a serpentine wriggle and came back with the attaché case in a matter of seconds and without any awkward questions.

'There.'

Trubbs lay in a patch of moonlight like a landed fish.

'Sh-sh,' whispered Josephine again, for he was trying to speak. 'I don't know what you're up to but I do know you're not in a fit state to do it. I'm going to take you to the san. Can you walk?'

The sanatorium was at the end of this corridor. A regular stream of boys passed through it, suffering from varying degrees of damage, but it happened to be empty at present. To offset this piece of fortune they had to pass Matron's room on the way, and Josephine was pretty sure that she was a hair-trigger sleeper. Matron would have to be told about Trubbs, of course, but not yet if it could be helped. Trubbs co-operated well. He took off his shoes. Josephine nodded approvingly, picked up his hat, wedged it, after consideration, on his head, took his arm and, with his case in her other hand, led him inch by inch along the dark corridor to the san. A fifteen-watt bulb served as a nightlight here and by the light of this she found a bed, pushed Trubbs on to it and, opening his case under the light, found him a pair of pyjamas. A packet of cigarettes rested on top of these. Where did *that* come from? Not the tuckshop, surely? Still, no time for speculation.

'Right,' she whispered, thrusting the pyjamas upon

him. 'From now on you're on your own.'

He had recovered slightly. 'I s-say, T-Tugnutt, w-what are you going to t-tell them?'

'I'll think of something.'

'B-b-but – '

'Don't worry. Lucky you met me, eh?'

'T-T-Tugnutt – '

'Sh-sh.'

' – you're awfully d-decent – '

'Shut up.'

Now, she said to herself, back in her bed, what's to make of this?

'Ah yes,' said Mr Johnson, nodding wisely, 'sleep-walking.'

'I suppose he was, sir,' said Josephine wonderingly, thinking how convenient it was that Mr Johnson, in his role of Housemaster, had to appear omniscient.

'Walking about the Lower Quad fully dressed and carrying a case. H'm. Something disturbing him, no doubt.'

'Yes, sir.'

'Anyway you did jolly well, Tugnutt. You showed initiative. We like St Chauvin's men to show initiative.' He caught himself up. 'Well! Girls too! Well! Girl!' He laughed his vicar's laugh.

'Thank you, sir.'

'Trubbs Minor. Not one of our successes. But I expect we'll lick him into shape in the end.'

'I liked the way you handled Trubbs Minor, Tugnutt,' said Porson a little later. 'Couldn't let the little tick sleepwalk all over the show. It'd give the House a bad name.'

'Thank you, Porson.'

'Actually, though, you should have reported the

matter to me. Just a tip in case anything of the sort happens again.'

'Are you suggesting', said Josephine, with dignity, 'that I should have come to your bedroom, wherever that is, in the middle of the night?'

She had not foreseen the effect of this. Porson went furiously red, held his collar away from his neck as if he were choking, and looked for a moment pitifully young and vulnerable.

'Oh, I say. Well, rather not. I mean to say, I didn't mean. I mean, sorry.'

I've actually scored off him for once, thought Josephine. More to the point was that she had seen Porson in just a flicker of a new light.

'I suppose you were trying to run away, weren't you?'

Trubbs was sitting up in bed. Matron said that he had a temperature and was to stay in the san for a day or two. He wished he could stay for the rest of his school life.

'Jolly clever of you to tell them I was sleepwalking. You're – you're awfully decent, Tugnutt.'

Josephine smiled at him. He was fat-cheeked and double-chinned and with his glasses off he looked like a startled baby.

'Well, you must have been very unhappy. Trubbs Minor – there must be a Trubbs Major. Can't he help?'

'Oh, gosh, no, he's in the Fifth. Fifth Formers don't have any truck with sprogs.'

'I should have known. Well. How are we going to stop you being unhappy? We'll have to think of something, won't we?'

The sweet feminine sympathy was too much for him. He blubbed. Two tears rolled down his cheeks. Josephine picked up a corner of the sheet and wiped his face.

'But, Trubbs, why on *earth* were you going to climb up the ivy in the Lower Quad? People only do that in girls' stories! Why ever didn't you just walk to the Main Gate?'

'I started to, actually, but . . . You'll laugh at me.'

'I probably will. Go on.'

'I – I thought I saw the Dorset Wolf.'

Josephine sat bolt upright.

CHAPTER FIVE

Soon, however, as a student of biology, she ruled out any superstition about boys turning into wolves. It was a physical impossibility. Trubbs, in a naturally nervous state, had seen a bush or a shadow or the porter's dog. And yet whenever she saw Mr Victor, looking for aye as if he were plumbing the dark recesses of the human psyche, she could not repress a pang of doubt.

The news of Trubbs Minor's sleepwalking was soon known to everyone in the school, with the single exception of the Headmaster, who kept himself to himself in a way that made the life of Fanshawe-Smith, now Brother Bartholomew, look positively convivial. It is likely that many a boy had gone through his whole school life without seeing him at all. He was, thought Josephine, like the three wise monkeys in one, although less pleasing to look at.

She did, by a rare chance, once meet him on the stairs.

'Ah, Jocasta. How are you getting on?'

'Josephine. Very well, thank you, Uncle.'

'Josephine, of course. Good, good.'

Getting on? Not well at all, if the truth were told. She had won the approval of a handful of people but the majority were somehow offended, as if she had broken some unwritten law in rescuing Trubbs and putting him

to bed. Better to have let him sleepwalk on, over a cliff if
need be, than do what she had done. She had breached
their comfortable right to treat him as a Weed. Start
showing compassion to Weeds and you spoil everyone's fun.

Matron, however, liked Josephine more than ever.
She was 'someone to talk to', the only someone in view,
and this latest incident had shown her to be good-
hearted. So Matron did at last confide in her.

'I'm separated from my husband, Jo.'

'I'm sorry.'

'Well, he was impossible. He was the laziest man on
earth. He used to chop the firewood in bed.'

'Oh dear.'

'He was an intellectual.'

'Is that bad?'

'Oh yes. He kept taking up mad theories. For a long
time he was anti-jokes. He said that all humour was a
form of sadism, and that all progressively thinking
people ought to be wholly serious all the time. There
was a terrible scene at a party once. He was jumping
about, all red in the face and waving his fists. He was
shouting, "Just who the hell are you accusing of having
a sense of humour?" I had terrible trouble calming him
down.'

'He does sound tiresome.'

'And, then, he's been corrupted by this dreadful
Society.'

'I suppose everyone is, more or less.'

'No, this Society he's a member of. He went to their
meetings every week. They want to erase all middle-
class culture, you know, like going to symphony con-
certs, saying please and so on. He was indoctrinated.
He insisted on our drinking tea out of flower pots.'

'He sounds awful,' admitted Josephine.

'I miss him dreadfully.'

Josephine stared at her.

'He sends me a Valentine every year.'

'Oh! Couldn't you try to make it up?'

'We love each other only when we're separated.'

'That's sad.'

'Yes, Jo, but you'd think it sadder still if your bed was full of wood shavings.'

Going to her room that afternoon, Josephine came upon the cad Cardew emerging from the sanatorium. She bristled instinctively. He provoked bristling. His lips were full and sensual, his eyes lustrous and prominent, and he parted his hair in the middle. But he said, 'Good afternoon,' very civilly.

'Good afternoon,' said Josephine coldly.

'I've just been visiting the invalid.'

'Decent of you,' said Josephine reluctantly.

'Well, we're in this world to help each other.'

Josephine was at a loss.

'I've changed, Tugnutt,' said Cardew, as if to help her out of her perplexity. 'Good influence.'

'Do you mean Fearless?'

'Partly,' said Cardew, with a sidelong look. 'Well, yes, certainly I mean Fearless. He's made me see things in a new light. He's given me a new set of values.'

'Well, good.'

'Good for Fearless, yes.'

'And you,' said Josephine, more warmly. 'It's very nice of you to call on Trubbs. Not many of the boys would be so thoughtful.'

'The fact is, Tugnutt, this place wants a new look altogether.'

'I think you're absolutely right. I wish I could help.'

'You're helping a lot.'

35

Which was a charming thing to say, even though he said it in the insinuating purr that went so completely with his suggestive facial expression. How easy it was to misjudge people by their appearances! Why, Cardew showed signs of being a decent chap! And even if he were a former cad there must be a lot of good in him for him to be reformed, mustn't there?

She was thrilled to think that her presence might have helped towards it.

She told Fearless about it, stressing his own influence. He laughed and said, 'Glad to have been of service!'

'You're too modest! By the way, did you know that Trubbs Minor smokes?'

'The young bounder!'

'Shouldn't laugh about it!'

'Oh, a cigarette never hurt anyone!'

This villainous fallacy was generally believed in the 1930s, and one advertisement actually commended people to smoke a certain brand 'for their throat's sake'! But Josephine did not agree.

'It would hurt Trubbs. That kid has got asthma.'

'Live and let live,' said Fearless pacifically.

Sometimes he was just too easy-going. But a thoroughly good fellow, all the same.

Mr Cropper had been curiously subdued of late. His pupils were getting no sport from him and were even losing interest, like cats with dead mice. Anxiously, they stepped up the action.

'When Hamlet fought Laertes, sir, did he lunge at him like *this*, sir?'

'Sir, Pugh has just jabbed me in the stomach with his ruler, sir! Have I permission to hit him back, sir? Pugh, take that, you swine!'

'Sir, Bradley and Pugh are fighting, sir. Shall we separate them, sir?'

'May we bite them to make them stop, sir?'

'Sir, this lout has just chewed my finger, sir! Take that, Rodgers, you oink!'

'Sir, Bradley has sloshed me with his pencil case, sir!'

Inviting damage, 3A rioted all round Mr Cropper's desk in the gleeful hope that he would cut loose, at best with some weapon. He remained still, looking at them vacantly with his mild blue eyes as if they were irrelevant, and after a while they subsided, disgruntled.

In a short while the whole school became aware that Mr Cropper's deceptively mild appearance was no longer deceptive. It was as if he had undergone an operation to make him docile. What was the matter with him? They were filled with a sense of loss.

Mr Cropper kept his books in a cupboard because he was ashamed to display them on his shelves. His education was in conflict with his natural taste, which may explain why he sometimes spoke Shakespeare instead of Elise Bobbin when he was on the rampage.

He unlocked his cupboard, picked out *Girl Wife*, still his favourite, and opened it at random. He knew it by heart.

Lady Euphemia [he read] *walked across the priceless Persian carpet to the magnificent marble mantelpiece, on which she leaned her elbow and stood awhile in thought. She and his lordship were dining alone tonight, and therefore she had merely put on a tiara with emeralds the size of pigeon's eggs, two necklaces, one a simple collar of diamonds and the other rather more elaborate with rubies dropping from a huge centre-stone; some bracelets, earrings, and a brooch worth a king's ransom . . .*

37

(It was the policy of Elise Bobbin to bedeck her heroines with costly and well-kept gems, since this sort of glamour was lacking in the lives of her readers, few of whom, in this year of depression, could run to more than melon seeds slung on a piece of string. However, the thought in which Euphemia stood was rueful.)

'I married his lordship', she mused, 'in a madcap mood of maiden folly, never dreaming that my heart would be involved. But now – poor little fool! – I believe that I may be falling helplessly in love with my own husband!

'And he? To him I am just a frippery bit of muslin – an after-dinner jest!' Two further jewels in the form of tears hung from her long lashes. 'He flouts me, and spurns my company!'

Lord Ravensbourne came in, threading his way through the costly furniture.

'This evening, my dear, I shall be dining elsewhere.'

'Else . . . where?' panted Euphemia, paling.

'Where else?'

'I – I – could forgive you – going – anywhere – but there –'

'Ha! I hope I have not married a prude, egad! I married you for sport, but I'm damned if I'll be tied to your apron strings, curse it!'

'My lord – that is – the last thing – I wish –' faltered Euphemia.

'You falter a lot, don't you?' said his lordship. 'Try drinking a glass of water from the opposite side. Au revoir.'

Euphemia found a clear space on the carpet and sank down on it. The butler, Relish, came in.

'Oh, Relish,' she exclaimed piteously, 'am I so unattractive?'

Something like a tear stood in the old retainer's eye.

'Lord bless you, my lady,' he said, 'this ancient pile has

been a sunnier place since your sweet pretty face came through its portals . . .'

Mr Cropper paused in his reading. That last sentence struck him to the heart.

There was a young girl in the school. She was the first he had ever seen. Yes, yes, there were a lot of them about, but he had never *noticed* one before. This girl was exceedingly lovely. Her marcelled hair enfolded her head like a swimming cap fashioned in wavelets of old gold. Her voice was like a singing bird's. Her eyes were cornflower blue. And a rose, her mouth.

He had spoken to her. He had handed her a cigarette card. He started up in shock. Why had he done that?

He held his head in his hands. He had been behaving very strangely for a long time. He had been squeezing multitudes to death in his hands, he had been crumpling battleships like tinfoil, he had pushed buildings over. It had all been a dream, hadn't it? A dream filled with gleeful yelping figures. He now felt like one who has backed his car into a china shop and dreads inspecting the damage. Some of the gleeful yelping figures came into focus. He remembered attacking them.

'I'm going mad,' he whispered.

He was, in fact, going sane; but daylight also has its illusions.

CHAPTER SIX

Trubbs Minor had found a way of keeping himself in the san indefinitely – even, with luck, for the rest of his school life.

Matron took his temperature every morning. In our present austere times patients are all but hustled into the street from off the operating table, but in the 1930s they were kept in bed much longer, and Matron would not let a boy leave the san until his temperature was normal. Trubbs found that by drinking hot water he could raise his by a degree and a half or so. A few minutes before she came in with the thermometer, he applied his mouth to the hot tap in the wash basin and gulped a good pint. Matron would be puzzled and would shake the thermometer and try again, but the trick worked and kept him in bed.

Josephine was pretty sure that he was malingering, but what good would it do to drive him back to a regime from which he had tried to run away?

Trubbs was, unofficially, her first case. He needed help, both medical and psychiatric. There was this matter of smoking, for instance. For all the social approval it enjoyed, she was sure it wasn't good for an asthmatical boy of twelve.

'Where are you getting cigarettes from, Trubbs?' (Juniors weren't allowed out of the school grounds.)

'Er – the Mater sends them.'

'Nonsense.'

'Er – I've got some left over from the hols.'

'The holidays ended weeks ago.'

But he looked so cornered and defenceless that she hadn't the heart to press him further.

His needs were twofold: a good habit to replace smoking, and – although this was a real problem – some achievement to impress his fellow juniors and stop them calling him a Weed. Juniors could be impressed by strange things. She suspected that Pontifex, for instance, had enjoyed considerable prestige on the strength of his virtuosity with a mouth organ. But what skill could fat, short-sighted, short-winded and generally inept Trubbs Minor acquire?

Josephine was reminded of the Yo-Yo.

Those who can recall the year 1932 will confirm that the Yo-Yo was a craze indeed. The hula-hoop of the 1950s, the skate board of the 1970s, and the Rubik Cube of the early 1980s were as nothing to it. Not only the young but the elderly were caught up with it. Parsons, magistrates, and even undertakers were among its addicts. Bowler-hatted City gents played with Yo-Yos in first-class carriages on their way to their offices. Big London stores held demonstrations given by experts. A World Championship was held, and was even made the subject of a commentary on the radio, although as a descriptive spectacle the Yo-Yo is extremely limited.

At the first opportunity Josephine went impulsively out and bought one. Her father was generous with pocket money and she had spent nothing while at St Chauvin's, so she paid the enormous sum of twenty-one shillings for it, which was about as much as a junior clerk in a London office would receive as his weekly wage. It was a Rolls-Royce among Yo-Yos, of aluminium, not wood, and elegantly slim; its cord glistened and it rose and fell with a silken hiss.

But now, twenty-one shillings poorer, she saw the difficulties in her scheme. Merely to turn Trubbs loose among his peers with this bauble would be worse than useless. First, she had to make St Chauvin's as a whole recognize the Yo-Yo as an art form, and St Chauvin's was entrenched in its own ways. And then Trubbs would have to master it, and he was depressingly butter-fingered.

So for the time being she was baffled, and rued spending so much. She glanced in at Trubbs. He gazed myopically and complacently back at her. He liked it here.

In the corridor she encountered Porson. He was supposed to be responsible for her 'safe conduct', but in fact he worried her more than anyone else. His concern for her was so extreme that she almost expected to find him hiding in the bathroom cupboard.

'How is he?'

'Matron's still keeping him in bed.'

'Then the little freak is damned lucky.'

'*Lucky*?'

'Oh, he's out of it all, isn't he? Having everything done for him. I wish I were.'

'You'd like to be like *him*?'

'Yes, I would. Instead of carrying the can all the time. And for what? For *nothing*. For *nothing*.'

'But, Porson, you're House Captain! I should have thought – '

'You'd have thought wrong then. You don't know *what* I think. Or what I feel. And you don't care.'

Josephine looked up at him with a face of innocent inquiry. This, admittedly, was partly coquetry, but also

42

because she dared not risk anything more encouraging.

'Josephine – '

'Yes, Porson?'

'Nothing.'

'Oh, please excuse me.'

He looked at her with a kind of rage. But he had no words for his feelings. He was a volcano with a lid on.

'Where are you going now, then?'

'Physics.'

'*Physics*,' he repeated, as if the word disgusted him.

'Yes. I hope that's all right?'

'Have a good time,' said Porson bitterly.

'Well,' said Josephine to herself, 'whoever would have thought it?'

But as a matter of fact she had suspected it for some little time.

She reflected on the matter while apparently attending to the physics lesson.

Porson, of all people.

'Josephine,' he had said, hoarsely.

Yes, really. He had said Josephine and he had said it hoarsely.

The best of us are devious and Josephine now began to think deviously, indeed to scheme.

Porson was important. He had influence. Get him in on her act, now . . .

That would be manipulating him.

Well? Wasn't he made to be manipulated? Like the Yo-Yo?

Entering Matron's kitchen, Josephine encountered a man just taking leave of her friend. From the fact that he wore corduroys and a beard she deduced that he was an intellectual, and from the icy atmosphere she guessed that they were married.

43

'He comes every month to give me some money,' explained Matron. She watched his back from the window and sighed. 'He's a fine figure of a man, isn't he?'

Josephine met him again a little later when, exercising her privilege as a Sixth Former, she was on her way to the library in the town. He was sitting on a bench just inside the entrance to the school grounds.

'Ha!' he said, without preliminary (a characteristic of intellectuals in 1932), 'I don't doubt you've heard what a villain I am.'

'Er –'

'There's no need to be in awe of me. Sit down, child.'

Josephine hated being called a child. She sat down, frowning.

'Mundy,' said Matron's husband. 'Ernest Mundy.'

'How do you do.'

'How do I do? Ha! The truth is, I've been inveigled into a farcical egalitarian charade, and I play a clown's role in it.'

'That must be very trying.'

'You don't understand a word I'm saying, do you, child?'

'Mr Mundy,' said Josephine, in cold clear tones, 'you have just said that you have been inveigled into playing a clown's role in a farcical egalitarian charade. I understand your words, but I do not find them self-explanatory.'

'By Jove!' exclaimed Mr Mundy, and looked at her as if she were a sunset or a rare fish. He turned towards her, twisting himself into an attitude of considerable contortion. 'You are surprisingly intelligent. Well, what do you make of me?'

'I must say, you don't look as if you make many jokes.'

Mr Mundy laughed a staccato laugh. 'God! I don't

suppose I do! But do you know the truth? I love jokes. Old Time Music Hall. Chaps in boaters crosstalking. With a bit of dance routine.' He rose and executed a few shuffling steps on the path, finishing by balancing on one leg, his trilby hat engagingly doffed. He did it very neatly, but his face was so woebegone that it fairly brought tears to the eyes.

'I love that stuff,' he said. 'I'm a music hall comedian *manqué*.'

'But – ' said Josephine.

'And another thing. She'll have told you I'm lazy. I am. I don't deny it. But it's entirely against my nature. I am by constitution hyperactive. I was well known for it before I married. I was dynamic. Whenever I entered a room, a door panel fell out and the handle came off in my hand.'

'But – ' said Josephine.

'I try to resist seeming lazy,' said Mr Mundy. 'I take exercise, running on the spot with logs in my arms, but I always end up by running upstairs and into bed with them.'

Josephine wrinkled her brows. 'Why do you drink tea out of flower pots?.'

'I know, the tea all pours out through the hole. Why? Because in every field of life I do the reverse of what I want to do. I am really a true blue, right-of-centre worshipper of the upper classes. As a boy I kept scrap books of royalty. So what do I do? I join the SPN, the Society of Progressive Nihilists.'

'Communists?'

'Left of Communism.'

'You are really the opposite of all you seem to be?'

'Yes. Because of my wife.'

'Your *wife*?'

'She's forced it on me. She's forced an awful falseness

45

of attitude on me. She's compelled me to assume an alien personality. I go through life acting a role that is quite foreign to my nature. She doesn't know she does, of course. It's her unconscious desires at work.'

'Have you told her about it?'

'Good Heavens. If you understood women, you would realize the futility of that.'

'Well, *really* –'

'Ah, I know it's all very puzzling to one so young,' said Mr Mundy, with a kind of satisfaction. 'My case is an extreme one, that's all. Freud might explain it.'

'On the other hand, he might just walk away,' said Josephine, rising.

Mr Cropper was just ahead of her as she went into the library. He was acting in a strangely conspiratorial manner, glancing about him and slinking forward in a semi-crouch like Groucho Marx. As he passed the counter, the wretched girl already mentioned exchanged a grin with her fellow assistant and the two giggled.

This made Josephine cross. She felt that Mr Cropper deserved more respect. Keeping out of sight between the shelves, she watched him. He shuffled furtively about in the region marked 'Romantic Fiction', edging closer while pretending to ignore it until he made a swoop, snatched a book, and meandered to another section, where, in a judicious way, he began studying the spines of books on engineering. Josephine took her own book to be stamped (coldly eyeing the wretched girl the while) and went into the library foyer, from where she watched Mr Cropper through the glass window. In the airiest manner imaginable, he sauntered towards the counter. The librarian stamped his book and giggled again.

No one, reflected Josephine, ever treated Mr Cropper

normally. People either baited him or humoured him. How would he behave if one treated him naturally?

One might regret it. She was well endowed with common sense, and she knew that to befriend someone odd could land one in the predicament of Sinbad with the Old Man of the Sea, but she was also very strong-minded, and too young to doubt herself. When Mr Cropper emerged, holding his book under his raincoat with a stiff left arm, she went up to him.

'Good afternoon, Mr Cropper.'

He lowered his eyes as if she were accusing him and went very red.

'Oh! Ah. Miss – er – '

'Tugnutt.'

'Yes, of course.'

Josephine took a chance. 'Mr Cropper,' she said, 'you very kindly gave me your card a little while ago, but actually, sir – um, actually – you gave me the wrong one by mistake.'

'I know,' said Mr Cropper humbly. 'A cigarette card.'

'Well, yes.'

'It was not a mistake, Miss – Miss Tugnutt. In fact, I do not possess a visiting card.'

Josephine faltered like an actress who forgets her lines. Mr Cropper said, 'I fear I have not been in my right mind.'

Josephine still had no words. It seemed so wrong to be listening to the confession of this gentleman three times her age. Mr Cropper looked at her troubled young face with great compassion, and said gently, 'I hope I did not distress you. I would not do that for the world.'

She was frantic to reassure him, and she gabbled. 'You didn't, sir. Really you didn't. Mr Cropper, *everyone* in St Chauvin's is mad. There's just no one who isn't.' Heavens, she was making things worse. 'I mean, practically no one. In some way or another. I mean – '

'Only my type doesn't Fit In,' said Mr Cropper. He might be dotty, he might be a joke, but he was a gentleman and he understood her confusion. He smiled at her benevolently, and she felt positively glad that his age was asserting itself, putting her, in the gentlest way, in her place. 'Perhaps one day,' said Mr Cropper, 'I shall be able to explain it to you. Not now.'

'Mr Cropper – I didn't mean – Mr Cropper, you're not – not at all. I didn't mean – '

'Not mad,' said Mr Cropper mildly. 'No, as a matter of fact, I'm not. Not any more. But – ' and he glanced down at his left arm where it was squeezing the book, 'but old habits die hard.'

She did not understand him, of course, and he was content that she did not. 'Anyway,' he said, 'I need them, the old habits. I need the refuge of dreams, or I shall be in for another kind of madness.'

His look was humble and regretful and full of adoration. She stared at him in pity and dismay. Oh God, she thought.

CHAPTER SEVEN

The term 'agony aunt' was not in use in 1932, but if it had been, Josephine would have felt like one. Since coming here she had been showered with confidences and confessions, two of them within the last hour, so that the latest all but eclipsed the rest. She had not, for instance, thought much about Mr Victor of late. He had left her to her notes and gone off somewhere, perhaps to invent an invisibility drug or a way to make gold or possibly an antidote to lycanthropy. There was Mr Mundy's obscure dilemma and Mr Cropper's painful one. But these adults were beyond her reach. There was Trubbs Minor. She really should be able to help him but for the time being she was stumped, with an expensive Yo-Yo lying idle.

She toyed with the idea of asking her friend Fearless because he was known for his initiative and could be just the man to start a Yo-Yo wave in St Chauvin's, and set Trubbs on the crest of it. But she decided against it. For one thing, she suspected that Porson was jealous of Fearless, and although she recognized that this was mean of Porson, she did not wholly dislike it and was strangely reluctant to hurt his feelings. For another, she could not quite make Fearless out. He seemed to have no deep emotions. Perhaps, with his perfect manners, he hid them? He was as bland as a figure in an advertisement. (She pictured him in one, urbanely proffering a cigarette in a silver case: 'De Reszke, of course.') Would he understand her motives? She would have felt easier about him if he'd been bad-tempered now and then. But still, he was a good fellow.

Well: she could train Trubbs in the craft of the Yo-Yo and hope that the opportunity of using it would somehow present itself.

Trubbs was no longer in the san. Matron had pounced on him with a thermometer unawares, decided that his morning temperatures were not abnormal and had sent him back to work. His fellow sprogs, for the time being, treated him carefully. The legend of his sleepwalking and his days in the san had placed him in a special light, and with the strange code of their kind they warned one another to be gentle. But this wouldn't last long.

Josephine added to his mystery by making him her fag. She feared that this might cause a scandal but it didn't; the school in general had come to accept her and she was just another Sixth Former utilizing a sprog. The readiness of society to adapt to new phenomena is astonishing. Even St Chauvin's possessed it and Fanshawe-Smith, immured in Woebegone Abbey, might with hindsight have acted less hastily.

Trubbs fetched things from the tuckshop for her, and cooked her tea. It got around that Tugnutt, the sole student of Mr Victor, was using Trubbs in some scientific experiment, just as Mr Victor had used his pupils in the past. And *then* it got around that Trubbs knew something about the Dorset Wolf and, indeed, had seen it that night of the sleepwalk. 'Right into the Quad it came,' the Second Formers told one another, round-eyed. How do such rumours get about?

At any rate they were giving Trubbs some mystic

prestige and the sprogs wondered if, after all, the Beak *had* chosen him to meet Josephine on arrival and if there was, after all, some special relationship between him and the fascinating new Sixth Former. Meanwhile Josephine got him started on Yo-Yo practice. She did this with some delicacy. She produced the device while Trubbs was making tea and casually operated it. She was deft with her hands, and made it ride its cord in a quite hypnotic fashion. Trubbs was fascinated and went on spooning tea into the pot mechanically. She took the teapot from him, washed it out, and with, 'Here, like to have a go?' fitted the loop of the cord over his middle finger, which resembled an uncooked chipolata sausage.

His performance filled her with dismay. The opulent Yo-Yo was ballbearing assisted and beautifully adjusted, and would probably have worked even if it had been hung from an airing rail, but Trubbs managed to make it go wrong. On his finger it became gibbous rather than round. It skidded and grated against its cord like a tyre against a kerb. It rose in jerks and hiccups and contrived to bind up Trubbs's hand as in a spider's web. Incredibly, it tied a knot in its cord. He handed back the tangled mass.

'I'm no good at this, Tugnutt.'

'You could be if you tried.'

'No, I'm just No Good.'

'Everyone messes it up to start with,' said Josephine, lying stoutly. 'Come on, try again.' She held his hand this time and compelled the Yo-Yo into some simple drops and climbs. 'There, see?'

'I saw a chap in Selfridges in the hols, demonstrating one,' volunteered Trubbs. 'He was terrific. He was making it Walk the Dog, and do Spokes of a Wheel and Shooting Star and things. Terrific.'

'So could you, if you tried.'

'Oh no, he was an expert, a champion.'

'Were there many people watching him?'

'Yes, a colossal crowd.'

'You could have a colossal crowd watching you. I mean to get Yo-Yo started here. It'll spread like a forest blaze. You'll see. You could be champion of St Chauvin's. I mean it, Trubbs. You could get your School Colours.'

'Gosh.' He was stunned by the prospect. He tried the Yo-Yo again, by himself this time. It imitated the action of a bolas and lassoed his right knee.

'Never mind. It's a matter of practice.'

'You really think I – '

'I know you can.'

'You're awfully decent to me, Tugnutt.'

You want your head examined, Tugnutt, said Josephine to herself. Making Trubbs expert with a Yo-Yo would be like trying to make music by banging cushions together. And even suppose she did achieve the miracle, what then? Forest blaze! Probably not so much as a respectable damp squib. It was a hopeless idea.

Nevertheless she kept him at it, swearing him to strictest secrecy. He became more proficient, making the Yo-Yo drop and rise with elementary competence. His face would grow pink as he achieved this; his eyes gleamed through his glasses. Yo-Yo practice is the mildest of exercises yet she fancied he had lost weight. She made the most of this.

'Every day, in every way, you're getting better and better.'

'Gosh. Do you mean it, Tugnutt?'

'Certainly. You'd do better still if you stopped smoking. Nicotine is a narcotic. It dulls the faculties.'

'Gosh. Don't want that, do I? I'll jolly well stop, then, Tugnutt. I'll tell Fearless – '

He stopped and went scarlet. The Yo-Yo swished back up its cord with unusual vigour and cracked him under the chin.

'Fearless? What about Fearless?'

'Nothing.'

Josephine took the Yo-Yo away from him and faced him like a Gorgon.

'Trubbs! What about Fearless?'

'Nothing, Tugnutt.'

'Tell me!'

'It would be sneaking.'

'Sneak, then. *Tell* me!'

'Can't we just go on practising, Tugnutt?'

'You won't practise ever again unless you tell me. Now then, Trubbs. Does Fearless give you cigarettes?'

'Not give me, no.'

'Does he sell them to you, then?'

'Please, Tugnutt, you won't tell anyone, will you, please, Tugnutt?'

'You should know me better than that. So Fearless sells you cigarettes. Just to you, or to other boys as well?'

'Lots of other boys.'

'And what does he charge you?'

'Ninepence for ten.'

'Good Heavens, fifty per cent profit! Where does he get them from? The shops?'

'No, Cardew's father has a night-club. They get them wholesale.'

'Well, well.' Josephine sat down rather heavily. This explained much. She decided that she had always mistrusted Fearless. Too smooth altogether. 'Heel it out *nicely*, Eagles!' The hypocrite!

Trubbs was shivering, the point of his collar was stuck in his mouth, and his hair, which no one had ever noticed before, was standing on end. Josephine pushed him into a chair, made him a cup of tea and gave him a slice of fruit cake. It was some time before he began practising again but when he did it was clear that a weight had rolled off his mind, for he showed more spirit and made the Yo-Yo rise and fall fifteen times without a fault.

'Tugnutt, when are you going to get Yo-Yo started in the school? Like a forest blaze, I think you said?'

'When we're ready for them.' Heaven grant that she could, somehow, so that this hapless sprog would not be cruelly disappointed.

But that rotter Fearless! And that snake Cardew! Ah well, fate would overtake them in the end, no doubt, as it usually did with racketeers. Meanwhile Trubbs was plucked from the burning. Well, the smoking.

In those days there was the belief, centuries old, that women could not keep a secret. It was a calumny. Josephine kept the secret of Trubbs's Yo-Yo practice perfectly, but of course it gave itself away by degrees. Matron became curious about Trubbs's regular visits; so did Porson.

Porson was jealous. Of *Trubbs*? He was jealous of the very frogs that Josephine dissected for biology. She might have found this agreeable had he vented his jealousy just a little more openly, but he was Spartan in his reserve.

'Why are you spoiling that little snipe?'

'He's my fag. Sixth Formers are allowed fags, aren't they?'

'He goes about looking too damned happy. It's not natural.'

'I like making people happy,' said Josephine, rather smugly. She was beginning to like Porson, perhaps because he was so unlike Fearless. She looked up at him as encouragingly as a nice girl could within the bounds of modesty. He coloured and shifted his feet.

'Josephine – '

'Yes, Porson?'

'Nothing.'

Oh, this marking time! Would he, having managed 'Josephine', never get beyond 'nothing'?

Now that Fearless's depraved initiative could no longer be considered, she needed to be hand in glove with Porson to get her plan under way. But the time was assuredly not ripe as yet.

Matron had always had her doubts about the sleep-walking story. She suspected that Trubbs had been trying to run away. It was not unknown for St Chauvin's juniors to run away, but it was never admitted. The Headmaster forbade such tales. 'St Chauvin's men do not run away. The possibility does not exist.'

Eventually Matron taxed Josephine with her interest in Trubbs, and Josephine confided in her.

'He needs to be good at something,' she apologized.

'Mm,' said Matron. 'Psychotherapy.' Psychotherapy was a word newly in vogue in 1932, and had great prestige. 'You're a born psychiatrist, Jo. I wish you could find some therapy for my husband.'

Diffidently, Josephine told her of her meeting with Mr Mundy at the Main Gate.

'Well, that beats everything. So I'm to blame. Loves jokes. Loves lords. Loves action! The truth is, he loves theories. *All* theories, the madder the better. I wish you could find him one. If he had a crackpot theory to cling to, he might straighten himself out. Or twist himself further, I suppose. Ah well. But as regards young Trubbs – yes, you've got a problem there. I suppose if he did get any good at it he might give a demonstration on Open Day.'

'When's that?'

'Three weeks' time. They set a room aside for what they call Endowments. Trust them to call it something silly. Just once a year, the boys are allowed to exhibit their own hobbies and interests.'

'It sounds out of character for St Chauvin's.'

'I think it's really for the benefit of the boys who are going to try getting into Oxford or Cambridge,' said Matron vaguely.

'How do you mean?'

'Those places', said Matron, still vaguely, 'like candidates to have interests outside schoolwork, like medieval glass or greyhound racing. So St Chauvin's plays along with them.'

'Could Yo-Yo be an Endowment?'

'Oh, I should think so. One year, a boy demonstrated sword-swallowing and cut himself to pieces. Usually they're rather dull. Pontifex is quite sweet with his mouth organ. Could Trubbs get up to standard?'

'I doubt it.' Even so, Josephine did now see the glimmering of a goal. Open Day, she mused.

CHAPTER EIGHT

Mr Victor looked worried. If you think he had no right to, since he drew a salary for doing nothing, you do not understand the sufferings of genius. He spent nearly all his time in the room at the end of the lab, emerging only at brief intervals to fling himself into brooding attitudes.

Josephine, who had given up his notes as out of date and was working by herself with a satisfactory text book from the library, never asked him what was wrong, although from his stealthy glances she knew that he wanted her to. A battle of wills was going on between them. She longed, with a longing made stronger by dread, to know what was in that locked room; and he knew she did. He longed for her to question him on it; and she knew he did. But she had the passive strength of her sex and was determined not to give in.

She was in two minds about Mr Victor. She wanted, oddly, to protect him because she felt that in believing he had gone one better than God he was probably very much mistaken indeed, and with that sympathy that was peculiar to her she pitied his being disillusioned. It would be like seeing a child betrayed in its faith in Santa Claus. On the other hand she partly believed in his Monster, just as she partly believed in his werewolf. Common sense? Oh, common sense would dismiss it all. But she was moving in a male world where common sense, which she had always taken for her guide, seemed to play little part. A man-made monster, a man-made man: dimly, she recalled hearing of some such thing before. Fiction? Some old novel?

Mr Cropper, she reflected, taught English literature.

Mr Cropper was a changed man. He was very gentle, very sane; and he went about with a touching air of bewilderment. Blindly, unreasonably, Josephine felt responsible for the change. Blindly, unreasonably, the whole school felt the same. Since That Girl had come a lot of things had gone wrong. Chaps becoming monks. Swots writing poems. Sprogs sleepwalking. And old Cropper. No fun there any more. In former centuries they might have arraigned her as a witch. In a way, they still did.

If she were responsible she had no joy of it. She was innocent, in all conscience, but she felt guilty. It was not right to be holding this courteous old gentleman in thrall. She wanted to put herself in his debt, to make him feel superior to her. Some girls could have managed this easily, putting on an act of wide-eyed worship in the way that the Broadway gold-diggers hooked their millionaires, but Josephine was no actress. But here really was the chance to make Mr Cropper feel important. Respectfully, like a student, she could ask his advice.

She waylaid him in the Lower Corridor.

'Men who created life,' he said. 'Yes, there are several stories in the ancient world. Prometheus – Pygmalion – '

'I meant, more like science fiction.'

'Ah, you are thinking of *Frankenstein*, Miss Tugnutt. By Mary Shelley. Shelley's wife, you know. A very silly story.'

'Silly?'

'Dreadfully silly. Frankenstein's monster is eight feet

tall. You'd think that would make him conspicuous, wouldn't you? Not a bit of it,' said Mr Cropper, chuckling. 'He hides in a hut adjoining a remote cottage where he remains undetected for several months. He watches the occupants of the cottage through a chink in the wall and learns their language so well that he can speak it in a style indistinguishable from theirs. He also – still depending on the chink – learns to read. His books include Plutarch's *Lives* and *Paradise Lost*. He becomes widely informed in geography, metaphysics, and natural philosophy. He achieves in a few months what it took mankind, through the more laborious process of evolution, thousands of years – '

(It has taken me, Josephine heard Mr Victor saying, *six weeks* . . .)

'How did Frankenstein make him?'

'Ah! we never know. All we are told is that he "has succeeded in discovering the cause and generation of life". We are not told how this discovery was made. The author simply assures us that "the secret is too terrible to be told".'

'An easy way out!'

'Yes, indeed. It is a very silly story.'

'Why did anyone ever read it, Mr Cropper?'

'Because, my dear Miss Tugnutt, men have a great need for silly stories.'

He gave her a strange, pathetic look and smiled sadly.

'And yet, if it were not such a silly story, we should feel sorry for that monster. He longs to be good but mankind rejects him with horror. He is even denied the female with whom he wishes to share his lot.'

'Was Frankenstein going to make a woman as well?'

'At first, but he decided against it.'

'Mean thing.'

'Meaner still to give him life at all, my dear young

59

lady. Not to be born is the greatest good fortune. All his attempts to do good are spurned. At last he is driven to murder and revenge.'

'You do know a lot, Mr Cropper,' said Josephine humbly. 'Thank you for telling me.'

'Thank you for asking me,' he replied. It was the first time anyone had asked him a serious question. Josephine knew this, and felt that she had done him a tiny bit of good.

Did Mr Cropper himself have 'a secret too terrible to be told'? An undercurrent in their conversation suggested that perhaps he had. But before she could dwell on this question she was approached by Porson, who still shadowed her with morose and dogged patience.

'So it's Cropper now, is it?' he snarled.

(Yes, really. Snarled.)

'I beg your pardon?'

'Aren't you content with driving the whole school crazy without picking on the staff?'

'Whatever do you mean?'

'You know quite well what I mean.'

'Do I? You don't express yourself very well.'

Silence, in which unconscious sparred with unconscious.

'Josephine – ' said Porson hoarsely.

'Look,' said Josephine, 'this is the third time you've said, "Josephine", and each time you've said it hoarsely. Yes, really, hoarsely. And if I say, "Yes, Porson?" you'll say, "Nothing." Which doesn't get us anywhere. So this time will you please make an effort? Here it comes, now. Yes, Porson?'

'You must know how I feel about you,' he said shakily.

'Must I? What am I supposed to do about it?'

'Oh, nothing, since Fearless of the Fifth is such an attraction,' he said bitterly.

'He's *not*, you know!' said Josephine with animation.

Porson was surprised but not displeased. 'I thought he was. He's such a jol – '

'He's nothing of the sort. Oh no,' added Josephine quickly, for Porson suddenly looked hot-eyed, 'he hasn't made a pass at me, if that's what you're thinking. He wouldn't risk it. I'm the Headmaster's niece. In any case, that's not his style. A cold fish, is Fearless. And a hypocrite.'

'Why, what's he done?'

'I don't like to tell you. He might take it out on the sprogs.'

'Well . . . I know that things go on that I have to turn a blind eye to,' said Porson, and added with deep and sceptical gloom, 'It's the Honour of the House.'

At which point Josephine fell in love with him. He didn't really believe in what he stood up for so proudly. He was blindly loyal. His not to reason why. He was tall, slender and boyish, neither handsome nor unhandsome: decent, vulnerable.

'All right, turn a blind eye but don't be really blind. There are some things you should see. Like who cares for you.'

'Are there?' he whispered.

'Yes,' said Josephine, and kissed him lightly on the cheek.

They spent the next half-hour in an empty classroom sitting in separate desks, for they were both brand new to their relationship and very shy and, anyway, this was 1932. Josephine found herself comparing Porson to Matron's husband in that he pretended to be the opposite of himself. (Had she but known it Mr Johnson had suspected this; Porson Fitted In only too well for it to be natural.) Now that he had stopped Fitting In for the time being and had, as it were, given in, it was as if his true self had emerged tremulous from a particularly brittle chrysalis. He listened to the tale of Trubbs with unexpected sympathy.

'Trying to run away? He's got more guts than I used to have, anyway. I was always wanting to run away when I was a sprog. I used to write home every day begging the parents to take me away.'

'Trubbs', said Josephine, who had learned a lot about her protégé, 'tells *his* parents he's having a Topping Time.'

'Is he any good at this Yo-Yo thing?'

'Average-to-poor.'

'Not very promising. Could I help?'

'Trubbs would be thrilled to death if you encouraged him. What, a kind word from the House Captain? He thinks you're God!'

'Feet of clay,' said Porson ruefully.

'And speaking of God,' said Josephine, 'do you know what Mr Victor's up to?'

'You've found out a hell of a lot since you came,' said Porson, when she had told him.

You don't know the half of it, reflected Josephine. 'Matron says he's lonely,' she said. 'He worries me. He gives me mad looks and says mysterious things and sits all hunched up and broody. Oh, don't *you* worry,' she added, for Porson was scowling, 'Mr Victor loves Mr Victor. It's one of the great love affairs of all time. It began when he was born. But I think he's very clever, and I can't be sure he isn't on to something. You know about the boy who was supposed to turn into a wolf?'

'Lot of tommyrot.'

'They saw one in the Quad.'

'That was a dog.'

'Well, if you see an eight-foot man in the Quad, don't say it's just a man because it'll be one all right but not *just* one.'

'Surely you don't believe – '

'No-o. It's just that I don't like being kept in suspense. I want to know what's in that room.'

'I've got the key to it,' said Porson guardedly. 'House Captains have duplicate keys to everywhere.'

'Golly.'

'Can't just nose around, though. Bad form.'

'There'd be no harm in just looking . . .'

'Josephine, what are you making of me, since I fell into your clutches?'

'A jolly decent chap,' said Josephine, and kissed him again making it twice in the half-hour, a good score for 1932.

From now on Porson, in public, became more Olympian in his manner than ever, especially towards Josephine, looking past her as if she were beneath his notice. When they were alone he showed her the tenderest solicitude. She was a healthy girl and didn't need physical support but she found it agreeable. She had learned that his name was Andrew but she still called him Porson in public because Christian names at St Chauvin's were out of the question. He regarded her with wonder. He knew nothing of girls, and had been brought up to assume they didn't exist. She knew nothing of boys but her own instincts were a huge help to her. They both felt a dotty elation in each other's company. They were absurd. It was working fine.

Beneath his lofty exterior he was in spirit about eleven years old. He gleefully anticipated sneaking a look at Mr Victor's locked room, just as he must have looked forward to midnight feasts in the dorm in his sprog days. This delighted her. He was human.

Perhaps they all were? We do not, she decided, so much live in a society, as build one around us out of our own delusions. She herself, for instance, was by a process of selection creating her own ward in St Chauvin's. Curious, how the patients fell into place, a psychiatric constellation, without any conscious seeking them out on her part.

Yet outside her own image of their world another world existed. It was mundane, as you would expect a world to be. From eight to nine p.m., for instance, the masters dined in the masters' dining hall. She had never visualized them actually *eating*.

During that time Mr Victor's laboratory would be unattended. It was on the first floor of the building in which Matron had her quarters. This was a two-storey building, but the upper floor was no longer in use. This, Josephine reflected, would be convenient for Mr Victor if ever his monster did come to life in that he would be able to keep him in a cage already rigged up in one of the disused upper rooms, and perhaps poke buns to him through the bars.

And so the evening invasion of Mr Victor's laboratory was planned. Matron dined earlier than the masters, as did the boys, and for half an hour after dinner her room was open for them to visit her. That would take care of her; but there might be one or two boys about. Josephine left her bedroom window open, in the foggy darkness of the late autumn evening, for Porson to climb through and creep with her up to the laboratory by the staircase at her end of the corridor.

Porson reached her window, as Trubbs had done, by slinking round the walls of the Lower Quad, and slipped into her room. Cautiously, she looked out into the lighted corridor. A shock. Strolling down the corridor with his back to her was Fearless. He went past Matron's room at the other end and out through the one and only door.

The evidence suggested that he had come down from an upper floor. Perhaps he kept his store of illicit cigarettes up there?

Tell Porson what she had seen? Why make him needlessly jealous? She whispered, 'Wait. Someone leaving Matron's room,' and stood before her trembling fellow conspirator for a full minute before peeping out again.

All clear. They tiptoed up the shadowy staircase to the darkness of the floor above. She had a torch, but did not dare use it until they had groped their way through the bio lab to the very door of the locked room. She shone it timidly round this Bluebeard's chamber, exceedingly fearful of what horrors it might light upon. It revealed nothing, except the welcome fact that blinds were drawn over the windows. With as much trepidation as if she were setting off Mr Victor's Ray itself, she switched on the light.

The room was almost bare. No scientific apparatus, no hocus-pocus. But in the centre on a table was a long oblong box, wired up.

Porson looked stern and grim. He was shaking. She took his hand protectively.

'Come on,' she said. And together they crept to the table, steeling themselves to inspect whatever obscene compound of dismembered corpses lay within the box.

It was full of sand.

'Is this his monster?' said Porson.

'Must be. It's in a rather undeveloped state, isn't it?'

'Let's get out of here.'

They made their furtive way back to Josephine's room.

'*Josephine –* '

'You must go,' she said, disengaging herself tenderly. 'It'd be awful if you were seen here.'

'I love you.'

'Same here. Go now.'

He went obediently to the window.

'Sorry this turned out to be such a sell,' she said.

'Victor's been having you on.'

'Do go.'

Porson whispered good-night with pathos and stepped out of the window. She watched him tenderly and maternally as he disappeared into the fog. He needed more care than any of them.

She drew her curtains, switched on her light and sat on the edge of her bed in a turmoil of which Porson was only partly the cause.

Having her on? There must be several hundred-weights of sand in that box. If it were some practical joke, wasn't Mr Victor going to extreme lengths to bring it off?

Sand?

The box was wired up. A switch would be thrown, presumably, and the Ray would course through it. All the particles would swarm into human form, like iron filings drawn into a pattern by a magnet, and a man not born of woman would be created.

Oh, rubbish.

'He's mad,' said Josephine crossly, but without complete conviction. She tried to give herself up to thoughts of Porson but Mr Victor kept invading them and so did Fearless, and she was unable to keep them constant.

CHAPTER NINE

In order to conceal their love, Josephine and Porson cut each other in public. Nevertheless it swiftly became known to the whole school. Love's night is noon.

It even, by some form of telepathy, reached Brother Bartholomew in the closed order of Woebegone Abbey and made him wish that he had chosen instead to go to Africa and shoot big game, or else to stay at St Chauvin's and shoot Porson. A duel, something like that. He was an impulsive young man.

The school felt deeply betrayed. Nothing would be the same again.

One of the alarming signs of the change was that Porson was now being nice to Trubbs Minor.

'Trubbs!'

'Please, Porson, it wasn't me – '

'Who's accusing you of anything, you little dummy?'

'No one, Porson. Sorry, Porson.'

'Then don't jump to conclusions, you little bat.'

'Sorry, Porson.'

'You have been practising Yo-Yo.'

'Oh! No, Porson. Well, yes, Porson.'

'Make up your substitute for a mind, you little gnome. Have you or haven't you?'

'Well, yes, Porson.'

'Are you any good?'

'Oh, no, Porson. Not very, Porson.'

'Well, you've got to get good at it. Expert. Do you understand? You are to give an exhibition of it for Endowments on Open Day.'

'Gosh. Oh, Porson. Oh, gosh.'

'Don't splutter like a half-wit. From now on you will be excused rugger and every afternoon you will practise in the gym from one thirty till five. Tugnutt –' Porson choked slightly and croaked the name, 'Tugnutt will supervise you. Open Day is in ten days' time. If you are not proficient by then you will receive ten thousand lines and a public flogging.'

'Gosh. Thanks, Porson.'

'It's for the Honour of the House.'

'Oh, gosh. Yes, Porson. This is frightfully decent of you, Porson.'

'Cut along and don't stand there gobbling, you little ape.'

Porson's encouragement inspired Trubbs enormously. Although he adored Josephine, he had always felt that there was something secret and forbidden about her championship because, after all, she was – one must face it – a girl. But to be commanded by Porson and for the Honour of the House! Trubbs's pudgy features became leaner and took on a new dignity. His fellow sprogs looked at him with awe. They knew he was up to something of fearful import. Rumours ran riot. A favourite one maintained that he, under the tutelage of Josephine and Mr Victor, was going to turn into some kind of wild animal. And Porson was backing him. Consternation was felt over this, and had the boys had any religious inclinations they would have crossed themselves protectively whenever they saw Josephine. But there it was: Porson was backing Trubbs and you could get no higher than Porson; there was no higher height.

One's state of mind is of supreme importance when one essays a bodily skill. Fierce pride and daily practice were turning Trubbs into a Yo-Yo virtuoso. He made it Walk the Dog, whereby it descended almost to the length of its cord and crawled over uneven surfaces like a miniature tank. He made it do Spokes of a Wheel, whereby it flashed back and forth clockwise so fast that several Yo-Yos seemed to be performing at once. He made it do the Indian Rope Trick, perhaps the most difficult stunt of all, whereby it climbed vertically and slowly, until, at the height of its cord, it flipped back to his hand so quickly that it seemed to vanish like a burst bubble. Josephine was delighted. They practised every stunt in the manual and made up new ones. He finished every session in collapse, an exhausted maestro. She sustained him with quantities of glucose. His expression became other-worldly and exalted. Even his brother, Trubbs Major, who above all others ignored him, began to feel the reflection of his distinction as if he were the nonentity relative of a famous film star.

Mr Mundy paid Matron another visit, icily conducted, after which he stumbled brokenly away and she wistfully watched his going. Josephine had by now found out that he was the Associate Editor of a magazine called *Perusal*, for brows very high indeed. On this visit he left a copy behind for the school library.

Matron showed no more interest in this than a cat will in a stuffed bird, but Josephine glanced through it. Mr Mundy had two signed pieces in it. On page eleven appeared the following poem of genius:

i in my am-ness
cannot consort with
thee in thy thouness
him in his hisness
her in her herness
them in their theirness
this in its thusness

never
not ever
never
do we see i to i

Josephine preferred poems that rhymed, but she was taken with this one, and thought that the last four lines would make a better motto for St Chauvin's than the silly Latin tag (*Non Titsi sed Tatsi*) that currently adorned the school badge. Never do we see i to i. Alas.

Mr Mundy's other piece (page twenty-seven) was an article entitled 'Mickey Mouse: A Sex Symbol'. Mickey Mouse would not have understood it and neither did Josephine, but she was impressed with the title. Matron had said that her husband liked theories, all theories. 'If he had a crackpot theory to cling to, he might straighten himself out.' The shadow of an idea, tantalizingly vague, crossed her mind.

No, she warned herself, you mustn't overrate the Yo-Yo. It can't be a universal cure. It rises and falls, like stocks and shares. You can't ask any more of it.

She took the copy of *Perusal* to the library and on a seat on the terrace outside she ran into Mr Mundy himself, raincoated and scarved against the chill autumn afternoon. His trilby hat was tilted back and his gaze was on the middle distance, which is located at about gallery-level of a theatre. He looked as if he were about to break into a soliloquy, which, as soon as he saw her, he did, for he was not one to waste a soliloquy if he had no audience. He introduced it with a brief preface: 'I have these fearful dreams.'

Josephine suspected that Mr Mundy confided in everyone, including the milkman and the boy with the fish, but she pretended to herself that she was acting professionally, and sat down beside him with an inquiring expression.

'I am standing on a hearthrug, deep in thought. The hearthrug is Persian and priceless. The mantelpiece beside me is marble and magnificent. The room behind me is fantastic and fabulous. It is a profusion of mirrors, candalabra and furniture, as if the Lighting Dept and Furnishing Dept of an Antiques Reproduction store had been jammed into one room for a sale. Ostentatious? It is. I love ostentation. I am so deep in thought that at first I am unaware that I am standing on the cat, and am deaf to its terrible cries. After a while they induce me to look down at my feet. Oh, horror! The priceless carpet is a mass of decaying leaves! The mirrors are stagnant pools! The fabulous furniture has turned to rotting logs! The candalabra are fungus-encrusted creepers! Frantic, I struggle to escape this mosquito-ridden spinney! I cannot move! The cat adheres squashily to my foot. It is no longer a cat. It has turned to some loathsome denizen of the wilds! It burrows into the squelching leaves, drawing my foot down with it. The rest of my body follows –'

'Well, it would, unless you were a daddy-long-legs,' said Josephine.

'I sink deeper, deeper into the mire. I sink to the level of my chin. I wake screaming.'

Josephine had an inspiration. Mr Mundy loved theories. There being none to fit the bill that she could think of, she would invent one.

'Mr Mundy,' she said gravely, 'I think you have a Woodcutter Complex.'

Mr Mundy laughed uproariously. 'A what, you funny child? A Woodcutter Complex? Whoever told you that?' He shouted with laughter again, and stopped abruptly. 'A Woodcutter Complex?'

'I think . . .' said Josephine, and thought quickly. She was wearing a fawn-coloured, fur-bottomed overcoat, a cloche hat and a fox fur, which she pulled close round her neck, peeping at him over it. She looked as delectable as a girl on a chocolate box. 'I think,' she said, with pretty hesitation, 'the idea is that woodcutters have always been connected with, well – *peasants* – *poor* people – you know, hewers of wood and drawers of water – '

Mr Mundy nodded, his eyes fiery with interest.

'Er, well – '

She was wondering how on earth to go on, but he took over with a rush of words.

'By God, you may be right. Out of the mouths of babes and sucklings, eh? A Woodcutter Complex! Yes, yes, I recall the theory. I have been indoctrinated with working-class sympathies against my will. I identify with woodcutters, the symbol of the poor! I dream of wealth and luxury, but my complex turns everything to stagnant pools and – and – '

'Rotting leaves.'

'Exactly. And fungus-encrusted logs. My complex overrides my natural inclinations. It really is most interesting that my identification with woodcutters is carried right into the region of my sexual life. Thus, I chop wood in bed.'

'Yes!' said Josephine, delighted. She hadn't thought of that.

'You poor child, how can you understand all this?'

'I think I can, Mr Mundy, now that you have explained it so clearly.'

'You are a clever little girl but you must not worry if all this is above your head because you are not old enough to take it all in, you know. A Woodcutter Complex . . . Yes . . . Freud? Jung? Adler? . . . One forgets these things.' He leaned forward, elbows on knees, and clasped his head in his hands. 'Ah, but what's the cure? How can I realize my comic self? How can I regain my natural dynamism? How can I admire the upper classes without guilt?' He smiled sadly at her. 'But there, don't you trouble your pretty little head. I'm afraid all this is beyond you.'

He gave her pretty little head a patronizing pat and went his way. Josephine went her way too, to watch Trubbs at his practice. She became lost in thought. It was not enough to say that life was stranger than fiction. Life *was* fiction. Everyone made up his own world as he went along.

Wait, though. Tell that to someone with toothache!

Still . . .

She was so lost in thought that she collided with the gym door.

Having spent a while with Trubbs Josephine went to the town, ostensibly to renew her library book but really for a tryst with Porson, who like herself had the next hour free. They were 'free' in a strictly limited sense. Before they had fallen in love, Porson had seen fit to talk to her openly. Now they were like resistance fighters under an occupation. Porson wore a tragic look as if this were their last farewell before facing a firing squad. They clung to each other in an arbour in the park and parted with broken whispers and a sorrowful stare. Deep and heavy was their love.

She did then in good faith go to the library and once again came upon Mr Cropper, who was also behaving like a conspirator, sidling round the Romantic Fiction shelves as if he meant to take them by surprise. She was pleased to see him. She had no qualms about him now. To be the object of an old man's desire could be most uncomfortable but Mr Cropper was a gentleman, which made him safe, and it was sweet.

But was he 'cured'? She watched him as he slunk to and fro. Why that clandestine manner?

Having an as yet undaunted faith in her own awful power, she went and stood by his side.

'Good afternoon, sir.'

A blush of guilt and shame spread over his face. It was as if she had caught him robbing a safe. He had three books under his arm and tried to hide them under his raincoat. She glanced at the shelves from which they came and was puzzled. Elise Bobbin, Deborah Cartilege – nothing under-the-counter there, nothing to be ashamed of.

'I read these myself sometimes,' she remarked helpfully.

It didn't help. Mr Cropper gazed at her in sorrow and dismay. With blind inspiration she recalled Mr Mundy's highly intellectual essay on Mickey Mouse.

'But I suppose in your case, sir, you're making a study of them.'

This was straw to a drowning man. 'The sort of thing they print in *Perusal*,' she added.

Mr Crooper blushed again, this time in relief and gratitude. 'Yes, exactly,' he stammered. 'A study. An academic study. Yes, indeed.'

'It would be above my head,' said Josephine modestly.

Mr Cropper drew himself up. He no longer looked

74

hang-dog. The face-saver had worked. But whatever he was going to reply was checked by the librarian, who gave their whispering a frown of disapproval from her desk; and Josephine decided that it was a good time to leave him. She smiled and nodded and went out, but he overtook her in the foyer.

'That was very kind of you, my dear,' he said.

CHAPTER TEN

Mr Cropper had said, 'Men have a great need for silly stories.' This impressed Josephine very much. If there were none to hand they'd invent one. In a closed world like St Chauvin's rumours thrived. The latest one concerned the Dorset Wolf, which was acquiring fantastic details. Trubbs Minor had seen the Dorset Wolf. He had come face to face with it in the Quad. It had spoken to him. With its long tongue flapping over its grinning teeth, it had said, 'I say, old chap,' in a voice which issued from its throat, with an echoing note as from a second-hand loudspeaker. It had held up a paw to detain him, and he had seen that it was not a paw but a human hand.

Quite apart from the absurdity of believing that a human boy could turn into a wolf, against the rules of nature, the story was obviously flawed. Trubbs was supposed to have been sleepwalking. If he had seen the wolf in his sleep, it was a dream. So had he been awakened by it, looked at it, human hand and all, and then fallen asleep again? Too ridiculous.

But no one reasoned like this. No one wanted to. Everyone *wanted* to believe the tale. And Trubbs, let it be admitted, did nothing to disillusion them. He was mysterious in the face of their questions with a masked and knowing smile.

'Well, he's having the time of his life,' said Porson. 'You can't blame him.'

The change in Porson was amazing. He spoke differently. He acted differently.

'Jolly good, Trubbs,' he exclaimed, while watching Yo-Yo training with Josephine.

A leaner, more confident Trubbs flushed and replied, 'Just a lucky fluke, actually, Porson.'

'Oh, rot, man. It was jolly neat.'

At the earliest opportunity, Josephine embraced him.

'I love you. You're doing *wonders* for Trubbs.'

'Must encourage the kid.'

'I'm so glad you think so. I love you.'

She tackled him on the subject of the wolf.

'Did a boy disappear or not?'

'He didn't disappear, he just left rather suddenly. He went to join his parents in India.'

'What was his name?'

'Woolf, funnily enough . . . But you don't believe this rot, do you? I like your leading me astray but there are limits.'

'No, of course not. But it's funny that people all over the place say they've seen it, people who've never heard of St Chauvin's.'

'One tale feeds another.'

'Has anyone ever asked Mr Victor himself about it?'

'It's difficult to speak to him. One doesn't know what to say. And most of the school are scared stiff of him. Funny, isn't it, old Cropper can swipe them with axes and they revel in it, whereas Victor just has to look at them and they're in a blue funk.'

'Mr Cropper doesn't swipe people any more,' said Josephine.

'No, that's a fact, he doesn't. And you're behind that, somehow, aren't you? Just what are you up to?'

'Up to? Nothing.'

'You are. You're changing people.'

'Well, at least it's into lambs not wolves,' said Josephine.

Porson, as Mr Johnson had said, knew the old school pretty well and kept his head when all about him were losing theirs, and Josephine was glad of his sturdy common sense when there was so much crying of 'wolf, wolf' (or perhaps 'Woolf, Woolf') going on. And yet deep down inside her a niggling doubt, which might be feminine intuition, persisted. Mr Victor had a belief in himself that was not to be laughed off.

Suddenly she understood why he was preparing to make a man out of sand. He thought he was God. Or as good as. She was faintly horrified.

It was very presumptuous of him, of course. But what had caused it? Was it possible that he had some rare gift that was too strong for him and had demented him but was nevertheless potent and real?

Porson had said that she was changing people. So, in all innocence (with just a bit of scheming), she was. But not Mr Victor. With him she was not Trubbs Minor's goddess nor Mr Cropper's dear young lady nor Mr Mundy's funny child. He had spoken to her so confidentially because he was so full of himself that he had to speak to someone, to the porter's dog if it had been there in her place. He was obsessed.

She wondered – but this was wild guesswork – whether Fearless of the Fifth was in any way in league with him. Once or twice she had thought she heard footsteps outside her room, light as a ghost's, and some instinct suggested that they might be those of Fearless. She had peeped cautiously out but had seen no one. Going upstairs to the upper rooms? Did he keep his illicit store of cigarettes there? Surely they didn't need that much storage? What then? What was his game?

She had never mentioned the cigarette trade to him. For Trubbs's sake she had not. On the surface they were still on good terms. But Fearless knew she had found him out. Why wasn't he worried? Couldn't she, the Headmaster's niece, blow the gaff to the highest authority and get him expelled? But she wouldn't, of course, and Fearless knew she wouldn't. He remained as bland as ever. He had a master criminal's nerve.

Oh, well, thought Josephine, don't worry your head with what doesn't concern you. Trubbs needs your care. Open Day had nearly arrived.

During the past few days Porson had been establishing Yo-Yo as an art form in St Chauvin's. He was uniquely placed to do this. Whatever he did, the House copied. Lolling among his peers in the tuck shop, he had nonchalantly produced a Yo-Yo, operated it briefly, and returned it to his pocket. He could do this without loss of dignity because in 1932 the Yo-Yo (see references, above, to City gents in trains, undertakers, etc.) was universally accepted. The sprogs, crowded at the other end of the tuck shop, were stunned, so that they stood with their jam doughnuts held motionless, half-way to their beastly little mouths. A stir went round the whole assembly. The next day Yo-Yos appeared everywhere: a rash of them.

Such a craze did they become that Josephine even feared that some boys, more naturally talented than Trubbs, might steal his thunder. Watching him again, however, she was reassured. Long hard practice had put him in a class of his own. It had also made him cut his Yo-Yo finger, which was now no longer sausage-like but showed the definition of the bone. She made him a finger-stall of thin black leather. This, by chance, was a master-stroke. It gave him an air of dedicated professionalism. He had added another trick to his repertoire now, which he called 'Hurdling'. He arranged a line of tumblers on a table, and made the Yo-Yo take a preliminary run up to it, as with Walking the Dog, and then hop over each one in turn. It was extremely difficult and most spectacular. She was proud of him.

But where were the Yo-Yos coming from, that were being confiscated in clutches during lessons and practised on by masters in the Staff Common Room? They were especially prevalent among the sprogs, who weren't allowed to go to the town. Surely their parents weren't sending them by post? So many? So soon?

She watched the sprogs in the Quad at break with Yo-Yos swooping and zooming everywhere so that they resembled pistons operating the little boys like dummies. Fearless happened to pass.

'This Yo-Yo craze is sweeping the school,' he remarked.

He was as affable as ever but a trifle self-conscious, knowing that she saw through him; and, of course, the remark was superfluous. But Josephine, in a flash, guessed the source of the supply. Why hadn't she thought of it before? Fearless must be buying them at two bob a head, and selling them at a profit of threepence or sixpence each.

Was that why he kept creeping upstairs in 'her' building? It might well be. She was even moved to creep upstairs herself to try the doors of what used to be dormitories along the bleak stone corridor, but every one was locked. Porson might have the keys, but why bother him? What good would it do? She contented herself with marvelling at the discreet way in which Fearless must be distributing the Yo-Yos and left it at that.

She did, however, resolve that if Mr Mundy should happen to come upon a scene of Yo-Yos in her presence, she would comment casually on their sex symbolism. He'd fall for that one, hook, line and sinker.

('What's "sinker"?' she asked Porson.
　'What?'
　'You know, hook, line and – '
　'Oh. It's a fishing expression.'
　'Well, yes.')

Preparing for Open Day reminded Josephine of getting out the old boxes of tinsel and paper chains for Christmas. She felt quite indignant at the *ordinariness* of St Chauvin's display. Why, it was just like any other school's.

Mr Cropper's room, for instance, was festooned with utterly boring charts of the life of Shakespeare, and pictures of Robert Louis Stevenson in the South Sea Islands, and cartoons of Chaucer's pilgrims on the way to Canterbury. Selected essays by his pupils were exposed on the desks. Josephine wondered however they had come to be written, considering what his classes were like. Perhaps they weren't real at all, like the chocolates in shop windows. There was even a poem by one Hopkins of the Fourth, something about 'Ling'ring in some long penumbral noon'. No, that couldn't be real.

Mr Victor's room, she surmised, was going to set him a problem. Not a bit of it. He, too, had his stock of paraphernalia. Spreadeagled frogs and eviscerated rabbits decorated the tables. It seemed that he taught anthropology as well as biology, though goodness knew to whom, and there were pictures of apes on the walls, Neanderthalers looking morose at the mouth of a cave and a creature called Homo Sapiens, erect against a painting of dawn, and looking (in view of his record) excessively complacent. He didn't know Mr Victor was planning to replace him.

On the morning of Open Day itself the school seemed deserted, as though all the boys had been driven underground. Josephine killed time, a bundle of nerves on account of Trubbs's impending afternoon performance, and came upon Mr Cropper alone in his room, sitting there in a trance of inept surrender. When he saw her he looked so startled and guilty that she could not pretend she had not noticed.

At such a moment any other nice, kind girl would have said something like, 'Mr Cropper, is anything wrong?' But what Josephine said was, 'Nothing's wrong, Mr Cropper. It's all right.'

He looked at her pitifully. He was the most defenceless creature she'd ever known.

She understood him. She knew that it would be no good keeping up the pretence that he was 'studying' romantic fiction for a thesis. That had been just a convenient improvisation. She knew that it was enough of an obsession with him to have driven him mad for a spell and that when she left St Chauvin's, and the shock of their acquaintance faded, it would overtake him again.

She said, with sudden inspiration, 'You ought to write them, Mr Cropper.'

His lip trembled. He repeated in a dry and shaky voice, 'Write them?'

'You've read a terrific lot of them, haven't you?'

Inspired guesswork, this. But he nodded, capitulating.

'Hundreds.'

'There you are, then. You've really studied the

subject.' (Just a flash, here, of the old pretence.) 'But now you ought to put it to use. You're very good at English.'

'Good gracious me. How did you know that, Miss Tugnutt?'

She didn't. 'Well of course you are,' she said.

'At school I was. I used to write stories and sketches for the school magazine and the like. They were very highly commended,' said Mr Cropper earnestly. 'But then I went to university and I became a teacher and I – I lost the will to write things of my own, somehow . . . *Write* them! . . . Oh, but – ' The enormity of the idea overcame him. He blushed crimson.

'Under a pen-name,' said Josephine.

He took heart. 'Pen-name. Good gracious. What sort of name would you – '

'Penelope Waynefleet,' said Josephine, 'or perhaps Angela Greaves.'

'Upon my soul. Which do you prefer?'

'I think Angela Greaves. Neater, isn't it?'

'Oh but my dear Miss Tugnutt – really – '

'Mr Cropper, it didn't seem such a strange idea to Deborah Carthorse – '

'Cartilege.'

'Cartilege. Or Elsie M. Dingle. Did it? They're doing very well out of it.'

'Is not publication exceedingly difficult to achieve?'

'I believe it is, Mr Cropper. I think you have to paper your wall with rejection slips. I don't know what you do if editors start taking your stories when your wall's only three-quarters papered.'

'My dear Miss Tugnutt.' Mr Cropper laughed, perhaps for the first time in years. 'My dear young friend. You're putting ideas into my head.'

'They ought to come out on paper, Mr Cropper.'

She leaned forward, suddenly deadly serious, in the unnerving way she had used to hypnotize Trubbs.

'Mr Cropper, you *must*. It's most important. You *must*!'

He turned pale. 'I understand what you mean,' he said. 'I'll try.'

Trembling a little at the audacity of her advice, praying that she had not condemned Mr Cropper to heartbreak and despair, Josephine perambulated the dead school, which resembled not so much a museum as something *in* a museum, until the first trickle of parents arrived and life stirred again. Soon a buzz began, which became a roar as in the gruesome cocktail parties she had sometimes been forced to attend with her parents. Boys became encumbered with jokey fathers and solicitous, inquisitive mothers. They loathed with grim horror this exposure of their parents in all their degrading limitations, and shuffled about mumbling and shamefaced in an agony of embarrassment. If Woolf had really become a wolf at the previous function, she reflected, he had chosen an ideal occasion to make his escape.

Some curious glances were directed at her. She ignored them with the feminine composure of which she was already mistress. The one person who did not glance at her, but looked through her as if she were invisible, was Porson himself, who occasionally passed her as they went the rounds. They kept up their icy indifference in public. It fooled no one, but it was their only protection. They were too hot to act naturally. Her knees shook at the thought of eventually getting him alone. He was in an even worse state. A rabid jealousy devoured him whenever he saw anyone looking at her or looking at the place where she had just been. Even her uncle, the Headmaster, was murdered in Porson's heart as, sauntering among the crowds as though he were an ordinary mortal, he paused to say something to her and rested his hand on her shoulder.

Now and then she returned to the bio lab, as its sole pupil representative, and answered a few silly questions. Mr Victor was there, gaunt and motionless at his desk, but no one approached him. Porson was right, it was difficult. People kept away as they would have done from the live rail at the station. For most of the time the lab was empty, and just before lunch, ejaculating, 'Ha!' or perhaps, 'Bah!' Mr Victor retreated into his inner room and locked the door. Josephine did not see him again.

CHAPTER ELEVEN

'Endowments' began at three p.m., in a row of rooms in the main building. The first two were given up to exhibits, models of the Schneider Trophy plane, Sir Malcolm Campbell's Bluebird and the like, and cases of butterflies and paintings – St Chauvin's acknowledged the visual arts. The third room was given up to performances. A cluster of boys had collected in an anteroom, nervous as beginners auditioning for a film. Pontifex of the Fifth was there with his mouth organ. He was cool; he was an old hand. His prestige in the school was a comment on its arrogance. St Chauvin's was a high-class school and the mouth organ, not yet given status by Larry Adler, was a decidedly back-street instrument, yet it was given grace simply because a St Chauvin's man chose to play it. In the same way, a duke could wear a cloth cap.

Trubbs Minor was there, his Yo-Yo in his pocket. Even now, his schoolfellows did not know what 'endowment' he was going to display. Most of them expected something sinister. Josephine could be seen in the big room with the visitors and rumour linked her with Trubbs and Mr Victor. Porson was there as master of ceremonies. His secret collaboration in the training of Trubbs would have done credit to a master spy.

In the few weeks that he had been practising, Trubbs

seemed to have grown taller. This was an illusion; in fact, he was just thinner. Some dormant self-respect had asserted itself and put lines into his face and figure where there had been flabby curves. He commanded attention. He sat quietly waiting his turn.

Muggeridge of the Third did some conjuring tricks with scarves and a pack of cards, turning his back on the audience rather frequently and having twice to start a trick over again. Paisley-Paisley played 'Demande et Réponse' on the piano, attended by the audience with glum goodwill. Trubbs was third.

He fitted on his finger-stall with almost ominous deliberation, like a gun-fighter about to kill, and began dunking the magnificent Yo-Yo up and down. He did this twenty, thirty times, so that the audience began to wonder what merit was in this act. Then, when the Yo-Yo reached his hand, it crawled up his arm and on to his shoulder and halfway down his back. Regaining his hand, it began shooting out round the clock, so fast that it looked as if it were being fired from a gun, its cord like so many steel rods. He made it Walk the Dog and Loop the Loop and Hurdle. He did the Indian Rope Trick. He had more command of it than the pianist had had of his own fingers. The Paganini of the Yo-Yo was Trubbs.

'That'll take some beating,' remarked Porson, as the act ended.

If his Majesty King George the Fifth had declared in public that he favoured a certain brand of cigar, if Rockefeller had indicated his preference for something on the Stock Exchange, the effect could not have been more striking than the effect on the boys of St Chauvin's of a public word of praise from the Captain of the House. Trubbs was made. The acts that followed were suffered rather than enjoyed and even Pontifex, who came last to render a medley from *Tea for Two*, was an anticlimax.

That evening, when it was all over, Porson walked out of the Quad and along the path to the Main Gate. A little way along he stuffed his cap into his raincoat pocket and, after a long, unhurried look round, left the path for a narrow track into the woods. By the light of the moon he worked his way to an old oak tree, and waited.

Five minutes later Josephine, the fox fur about her neck and a cloche hat covering her waves, set off in the same direction. Reaching the same narrow track, she threaded her way along it and, removing her gloves, came face to face with Porson at the oak.

They held hands and gazed into each other's eyes. There was less physical contact between them than there is with the average couple saying goodbye on a crowded railway platform. They were young and shy and in awe of this new experience. They were much in love.

Tonight they both felt depleted and a little sad. Trubbs had been a great success, but what now? Only a few weeks of the term remained, and then Josephine would leave St Chauvin's. Would the bubble of her revolution then burst? She had sensationally changed Porson, but would that fade as time went on without her? Would he still champion crushed and timid sprogs? Had she really brought his true self to light, or just put a spell on him?

Lovers need continual reassurance. Porson needed it even more than she. He believed that the whole world must be in love with Josephine – how could it help itself? – and the thought of parting from her dismayed him. He would have liked to keep her locked up, preferably in a walled garden full of roses. Josephine had brought him to life – not since he was an infant on his mother's lap had he felt as he was feeling now – but with life came pain. He was jealous of every living thing.

He had heard of the treachery that lay in women's smiles. But as soon as he doubted her he was pierced with barbs of remorse. Oh no, not in her smiles. He gazed deep, deep into her blue eyes. Ah, but she was lovely. His was the first love in the world. He would die for her if he could.

What he said was, 'I feel a bit of an ass, standing here like this.'

'You do say romantic things.'

'I say, don't talk rot.'

They were silent for a while.

He burst out, 'Why do you have to go back to that school?'

'Because it's a girls' school and I'm a girl.'

'You'll forget me when you're with all those people.'

'What could be safer? Holloway? A nunnery?'

'See me in the holidays?'

'Yes, if I can manage it.'

'*Promise.*'

'Look, I can't absolutely promise, because I don't yet know what I'll be doing.'

'You could if you really wanted to.'

'Well, of course I want to.'

'I don't think you love me as much as I love you.'

'Yes, I do.'

'Promise, then.'

This dialogue was threatening to become circular, but now a new sound disturbed them. It was the patter of feet, accompanied by panting breath.

'It's the porter's dog,' whispered Porson uneasily.

'Too heavy.' The porter's dog was a fox terrier.

'Some dog or other, anyway.'

'Let's hope so.'

They clung to each other and peered about in the moonlight. The feet had stopped, but the breathing was oppressively near. Josephine whimpered and pressed her face into Porson's chest. She could hear the cannoning of his heart. He hugged her, more as if she were a kind of lifebelt than to protect her, and glared round over her shoulder. Nothing was to be seen. But if a well-bred voice with wolfish inflexions had called, 'I say, old chap,' neither of them would have been wholly surprised.

Then Porson remembered his high office.

'Get away!' he commanded in his most prefectorial voice. 'Get away at once! Do you hear?'

Was it possible that the Dorset Wolf, Woolf transmogrified, heard the voice of authority and obeyed? At any rate the panting ceased, as if the creature had obediently closed its mouth, there was a scurry in the bushes and then the sound of paws on the autumn leaves, going at a walking pace and possibly with a limp. Josephine felt compassionate, sensing that some creature sorely in need had been sadly turned away, but she still clung to Porson, and he to her, and they listened, rigid, as the steps retreated and died away.

'Fox, maybe.'

'Too big.'

'Big dog.'

'Yes, must have been.'

'We'd better get back.'

They edged their way along the narrow track, holding hands, till they reached the path.

'Shouldn't really go back together,' muttered Porson.

'I'm *not* going on my own.'

'No, all right. We'll go as far as the Quad, then you go ahead and I'll follow.'

'You were ever so brave.'

'Just a dog.'

'All the same.'

Comforted, feeling safe now, they went cautiously back towards the Quad, arms round each other, more on the lookout for any casual witness from the school than for wolf or dog. They had not gone far when they were stunned by a muffled explosion, a kind of evil punch in the air, from the direction of the school buildings. It was followed by a prolonged clinking and cracking of broken glass.

They hurried to the Quad and, separating, slipped into it. Boys and masters were pouring out from every direction and they mixed in with them unobserved. Porson pounded up to Mr Johnson's room and Josephine ran to her own room. Yes, it was in the Lower Quad, in the old building containing the bio lab, that the explosion had occurred. The ground floor seemed untouched but all the windows had been blown out on the first floor, and as everyone rushed to the scene with a confusion of yells and shouts and angrily barked orders and the frenzied squeaking of sprogs, they found themselves treading something gritty underfoot. Sand.

Matron seized Josephine by her arms.

'Where have you been?'

'For a walk.'

'Thank goodness. I thought you might be tinkering about upstairs.'

'Who –'

'Mr Victor, I suppose. I knew he'd kill himself one of these days.'

'Hadn't we better –'

'Stay where you are, Jo. Let the masters take care of it.'

Josephine had no choice. The staff and senior boys, admirable in a crisis, were already in well-organized action. They were momentarily delayed by the Headmaster, who had issued from his study suspecting a disturbance.

'Why are you gentlemen congregating here?'

'Explosion on the bio lab floor, Headmaster,' said Mr Johnson.

'Ah. There may well have been some such occurrence, but we must not hastily jump to conclusions. Was anyone up there?'

'Mr Victor, as far as we know, Headmaster. By himself.'

'Ah. Fortunately his duties are very light, so in the event of his being incapacitated – although we must not anticipate trouble – he will hardly need a replacement. Please report to me when the facts are known.' And the Headmaster went away, not displeased, because what to do with Mr Victor had been worrying him for some time.

Very soon all the sprogs were dismissed, under threat of expulsion and a public flogging (in reverse order) if they remained, and the staff and a few seniors ascended the stairs.

The door to the first floor had been wrenched askew and jammed the entrance, but Fearless of the Fifth produced a screwdriver and removed it from its hinges and it was lifted clear. The light bulbs in the corridor were all shattered, but Fearless produced several hand torches from his person and handed them round, and all made their way into the bio lab itself, the door of which had been blown right off. Here, all the light bulbs and windows were also broken but otherwise the damage was negligible. The door to Mr Victor's inner room, curiously enough, was still intact, except that one of its panels had fallen out as though Mr Mundy had entered by it in his dynamic batchelor days. Mr Johnson put his hand through the space and after some effort unlocked the door from inside.

Broken windows, light bulbs, etc., and an obscene tangle of blackened flex hanging in mid air. Thickly all over the floor was the sand which they had been trampling throughout this undertaking. It seemed to have been precipitated from a coffin-sized box, whose sides had been flung about the room but whose base, still on the table, retained a heavy residue. Blackened wires trailed from this structure, too.

Mr Victor was not to be seen. But stay: yes, he was. The old-fashioned room was some twelve feet high with beams across its ceiling, and from a hook in one of these Mr Victor was found to be dangling in the most ludicrous fashion, the hook through his trouser leg, so that he looked like an enormous bat.

Fearless mounted a chair and cut him loose with some large tailor's scissors, which he happened to have brought with him, and the others caught him gently as he fell and propped him right-way-up. He sank to the floor like an old overcoat and lay still.

By now an ambulance had arrived in the Lower Quad, Fearless having summoned it while the rest were searching, and Mr Victor was placed on a stretcher and carried out to the sound of the scrunching of sand. As they laid him in the ambulance he opened his eyes.

'I am Alpha and Omega,' he said faintly.

'Course you are, old chap,' said one of the ambulance men soothingly, 'but take it easy, because you're nearer Omega just now.'

Mr Johnson looked round the disordered room,

which the school porter and his assistants, summoned by Fearless, were clearing up.

'The ground floor's all right,' he said. 'Better look at the top one, to make sure.'

'Good idea, sir,' said Fearless promptly. 'I'll go.'

'Wait, Fearless. I'll come with you.'

'No need, sir.' And he dashed off, leaping up the stairs to the top floor like a chamois, to return in a few seconds.

'All serene, sir. No damage.'

'Hadn't we better check –'

'No need, sir. Everything in perfect order,' said Fearless firmly.

Mr Johnson hesitated, then decided to inspect his colleague before the ambulance drove him away. Mr Victor, having made his brief speech, had closed his eyes again, and was not to reopen them for some days.

'So ends Mr Victor's home-made man,' said Josephine.

'Well, what did you expect?' said Porson. 'The man was off his head. You're always telling me this place breeds loonies. Well, there you are. Crazy as a coot.'

'Yes.'

'You sound quite sorry about it.'

'Well, he'd be so disappointed if he knew.'

'Yes, but wolf-boys! Manufactured men!'

'Yes.'

'I believe you'd like to believe it all!'

Josephine looked submissive. In a general way she felt herself to be more practical than Porson, but in this case accepted that his male common sense must prevail over her foolish doubts.

'Oh no, of course not.'

'What *is* funny, though,' said Porson, 'is what caused such a terrific explosion. I mean, there don't seem to have been any explosives – dynamite, nothing like that. It's just as if he blew an enormous fuse. Must have been this special Ray of his, I suppose.'

'Mm,' said Josephine. Even now she could not wholly believe that Mr Victor's schemes were the nothing they appeared to have been brought to.

Porson looked at her anxiously. If she were anything but rapturously happy he always feared that he himself might be to blame.

'A good day, though,' he said. 'Wasn't it? I mean, Trubbs turning up trumps, and all that?'

'Oh yes,' said Josephine; but just a trifle listlessly.

CHAPTER TWELVE

'Trubbs Minor,' said Mr Johnson. 'What is his position in class?'

'He's bottom in everything, sir,' said Porson.

'Ah yes. Second Form work is not stretching him enough. He must be moved up.'

'He'd be out of his depth in the Third, sir.'

'Not the Third, Porson. The Fourth. It's hardly seemly that Trubbs should be Captain of a school game and remain a junior. Besides, the Fourth need some new blood. They're inclined to be over-academic at present. Not entirely healthy.'

'You mean, chaps writing poems and so on, sir.'

'Well, not to put too fine a point on it . . . Tell Trubbs to see me, will you?'

When Trubbs Minor presented himself to his House-master he was cool and collected and no longer said 'gosh'. He even appeared to be wearing new glasses of fashionable design, which gave him an efficient look. This may have been an illusion, however.

'You realize, Trubbs,' said Mr Johnson, 'that you are starting a new tradition in the school. You are the founder of a new sport. This will be unique to St Chauvin's, like the wall game at Eton.'

'Oh, I hope not, sir. I'm looking forward to challenging other schools.'

'Ah yes! Good point. Good man. Not wearing your school colours yet?'

'I'm picking up the tie this evening, sir.'

'Good. Mustn't be improperly dressed! Have you arranged any trials yet?'

'Begin this afternoon, sir.'

'Not letting the grass grow, eh?'

'It's a matter of weeding out the slackers, sir.'

'Yes. Good man.'

Trubbs's elevation to the new post of Captain of Yo-Yo had been caused by pressure from outside the school. His reputation had spread among the general public. A reporter fellow from the local newspaper had sought permission to interview him. He had been crushingly refused, of course. 'One has pupils,' said Mr Johnson icily. 'One does not have them interviewed.' A similar rebuff was given to the great store that wanted Trubbs to give an exhibition. But St Chauvin's was impressed with his impact on these vulgarians. There was no reason why the school shouldn't take advantage of the publicity, in a dignified way. And so Yo-Yo became a school game, and Trubbs its pioneer.

The news of his skill leaked to the world at large from the parents, who, leaving the school on Open Day, talked of little else. Desperate for their own sons to get on, they bullied them mercilessly: 'Why can't you do something like that? Aren't you sorry now that *you* didn't think of specializing in something useful?' They harangued the poor little wretches of younger brothers, booked for St Chauvin's in the future, commanding them to buy Yo-Yos immediately and practise like top tennis players.

Although the Yo-Yo craze had been sweeping the country for months, this latest development gave it special local interest, which in turn extended its mandate. Mr Mundy wrote about it in *Perusal*. Josephine noted with great interest that he did not treat it as a sexual phenomenon. He related it to Merrie England and argued that it compensated for a lack in a modern world starved of medieval revelry. She was not clear how he worked this out, but she was impressed with the change in him.

Trubbs collected his school colours tie from Matron's store and put it on there and then. It was of silken material, with slanting stripes of silver and purple. Josephine came across him as he went out into the Lower Quad.

'You look resplendent!'

'Thank you, Tugnutt.' He stood in front of her, looking earnest. 'Tugnutt,' he began.

'Yes?'

'Er – Tugnutt.'

'Yes?'

'Tugnutt, will you marry me when I grow up?'

'Yes, of course I will.'

'You're such a jolly good help to me, Tugnutt.'

'I shall be proud to devote my life to you.'

Her promptness flustered him. 'It wouldn't be just yet,' he said anxiously.

'No, of course not. You've got so much to do just now, haven't you?'

'Yes. Gosh, yes.'

'You must let me know when you're ready.'

'This is jolly decent of you, Tugnutt.'

'Don't mention it.'

And Josephine went on to keep her appointment with Porson.

Mr Cropper was typing the last few words of his first short story. He had drawn his curtains, locked his door and put on the light. Round his table he had arranged a dozen novels, all open at the last page, and with every word he wrote he consulted every one of them to keep in touch with the authentic style.

'My own,' he said tenderly, in deep and vibrant tones. 'My dream, my wife.'
'My husband,' she said –

Mr Cropper hesitated. How did she say it? Blissfully, passionately, breathlessly, weakly, feebly? Or perhaps it needed a different verb? She: panted, whispered, murmured, cooed, stammered, squeaked?

Finally he settled for leaving out the way she said it altogether.

'My dream, my wife.'
'My husband.'
She let herself be drawn within the circle of his arms.

Then Mr Cropper typed the title page: *The Fragrant Altar*, by Angela Greaves, 3,500 wds approx., and enclosing a stamped envelope addressed to Angela Greaves, Poste Restante, at the local post office, he sealed everything up and slunk out to post his contribution to The Editor, *Woman's Star*.

Mr Mundy was visiting Matron more often than once a month now. They seemed to be getting on better. They even went for walks together. They were not kissing again with tears, hardly that, but at least a kind of armistice prevailed between them.

'He's changing,' said Matron, perplexed. 'Jo, do you know anything about this?'

'Me? No.'

'He said you'd reminded him of some complex or other. He's changing.'

'How?'

'He's started wearing a blue tie for one thing, and then he's begun to make jokes.'

'Good ones?'

'No, terrible. The last time he was here he spent a lot of time fixing a cork on my hat – '

'He did what?'

'A cork. I thought it best not to notice. We went for a walk and he suddenly began dancing about and pointing at me. "I see they've put a stopper on you at last," he said, and stood there looking so worried that I felt sorry for him. He takes being funny so seriously.'

'Are all his jokes like that?'

'Some I can't understand at all. Whenever we cross a street he says, "*Sic Transit Gloria Mundy*". My name's not Gloria, it's Eileen.'

'It's a start, though,' said Josephine doubtfully.

Yes, it was a start, but was it good? Or was Mr Mundy simply going to be the same man with another lot of obsessions?

Which led Josephine to think about her other 'cases'. Trubbs? She had rescued him from a life of misery. But might he not get a shock when he left school and found there was more to life than manipulating a Yo-Yo?

Mr Cropper? All very well to tell him to write but literature breeds its own distress. How would he stand up to continual rejection and disappointment?

She felt guilty. Since coming here she had discovered new powers in herself. They came partly from just being a pretty girl, but mainly they came from a magnetism all her own. Had she really used them for good, or had she been indulging herself? Some of both, wasn't it? She could affect others, not altogether unknowingly, by a look, the tone of her voice, the posture of her body. Her formal dress, her prim manner, were in their own way provocative and she knew how to make them so. Josephine blushed in the solitude of her room. She felt guilty.

There was Porson. What was she doing to him? Last evening hadn't gone so well. Like an idiot, she had told him of Trubbs Minor's offer of marriage. She might as well have given him poison. Nothing she said could clear the jealousy from his system. At last she had become angry. Look, if he couldn't trust her with twelve-year-olds and sixty-year-olds and other people's husbands (for Mr Cropper and Mr Mundy had been brought in) he couldn't think much of her. They'd made it up at last, rather more demonstratively than ever before, but she was left with misgivings.

It was ridiculous, wasn't it? From starry-eyed elation to sombre passion to *doubt* in a matter of weeks? But in fact the joke of 'waiting' for Trubbs Minor had posed the question of waiting for Porson, and she doubted her constancy. There had been some zest in enticing Porson, the lofty House Captain, but when unmasked, as it were, he turned out to be anything but lofty. He was over-anxious to please. That in fact was why he was such a model House Captain. And in his anxiety to please her, and have her, and hold her, he could be rather tiresome. She hated the thought of breaking his heart. She foresaw that she probably would.

She could not charm everyone. There was Fearless. Nothing charmed him except money. But she believed that our sins find us out, and she was sure that before long Fearless and his crony would come to grief. No one but themselves to blame. Good.

There was Mr Victor. No, she had not charmed him. He was too charmed with himself. Poor man. She hated the thought of his bitter disappointment when he recovered.

But thank goodness she was in no way involved.

Matron knocked at her door and looked in.

'You're wanted on the phone, Jo. It's the cottage hospital.'

'Thank you for coming, Miss Tugnutt,' said the Ward Sister. 'He's spoken your name several times. I'm afraid you won't get much sense out of him but just let him talk, will you?'

'What exactly is wrong with him, Sister?'

'We're not sure. He's banged his head pretty badly, but it's not just ordinary concussion. He seems to have received some violent shock. Almost as if he'd been struck by lightning. There was some sort of explosion, wasn't there? No one can tell us exactly what that was.'

Mr Victor's head was swathed in bandages. With these, and the increased gauntness of his face, he resembled the monster Josephine had once imagined he was making.

'Tugnutt,' he said.

'Good afternoon, sir.'

'Only one with any intelligence.'

'Thank you, sir. Is there anything I can do?'

'Yes.' Mr Victor put a claw-like hand outside the bed and beckoned her, but the effort tired him and he lay back, stricken. Josephine sat by the head of the bed and waited. She could not help thinking that Mr Victor was always readily stricken, but Sister said anxiously, 'Easy now. Don't upset yourself.'

'Formula,' said Mr Victor.

'What formula, sir?'

'Formula.'

'Yes, sir?'

'Formula.'

'Yes, sir, but the formula for what?'

'Don't tax him, now,' said Sister.

'Perhaps you could tell me what the formula is,' said Josephine.

Mr Victor looked pained and resigned.

'Perhaps you'd better go,' said Sister. 'He must not overtax himself.'

'Yes, all right.'

Mr Victor clutched Josephine's sleeve in his emaciated hand.

'Formula.'

'Yes, sir.'

Porson had escorted her to the hospital and was waiting in the foyer in his usual distrustful state. 'Well, that didn't get you far, did it?' he said peevishly. 'What's "formula" supposed to mean?'

'How should I know? I suppose I've got to look for one.'

'Why waste your time on Victor?'

'Oh, look on the bright side. It'll keep me away from Trubbs Minor, won't it?'

Since the explosion, Josephine had read her text book in the school library. Late the next afternoon, however, when a bio lesson was due, she went up to the lab and began opening cupboards and drawers in a search for she knew not what. The broken windows and light bulbs had been replaced, the splayed frogs and rabbits, their insides full of sand, had been removed and the place looked derelict. Mr Victor's inner room, no longer locked, was equally barren. Only his white coat, on a hook on the wall, suggested that anyone had ever worked here.

The base of the oblong box, with a torn rim left from its shattered sides, was still on the table with its sediment of sand. Josephine looked into this. Were there indentations in the sand, as if some form had lain there? She pictured a statue coming alive out of its rock and leaving the hollow of its shape behind.

She left the bio lab, none the wiser for her search, and then the whim took her to go upstairs instead of down. Fearless had some business up there, she was sure. Yo-Yos? The demand had been met by now. It could hardly be cigarettes. Anyway, she ascended to the top floor and went through the swing door.

She had gone only a few paces along the corridor when she heard sounds from one of the locked rooms on the left.

Someone – some*thing* – was moving about in there. Josephine, facing the door, went cold all over and stood with staring eyes in terror lest it should come out and face her.

But no; whatever was in there was in no hurry to come out.

Probably she was letting her imagination overwhelm her common sense, but she could not help associating the occupant of this room with the hollow in the sand below, and if she had been a little less frightened she would have screamed. As it was, she dared not. She stood petrified, and in a minute or two her terror abated a little.

She had always pictured Mr Victor's 'man' as very heavy and clumsy. His movements would be brutish, with clumping steps as if he were wearing diver's boots. The sounds from the locked room suggested something moving lightly and easily. This caused her some relief, but only for a moment. She now pictured something swift and deadly. A violent shudder freed her, and she backed along the wall to the swing door, slipped through it and tottered to her own room below.

She drank a cup of tea and calmed down. She really had put a most preposterous interpretation on it! Fearless! It had probably been Fearless in that room! This thought – no matter what mischief he might be up to – came as a tremendous relief. She decided that her fevered head needed cooling and went out into the cool dark autumn afternoon and strolled to the Main Quad.

'Good afternoon,' said a cultured voice. It belonged to Fearless.

'Where have you come from?' demanded Josephine shakily.

'Geography, actually,' replied Fearless, surprised. 'Why?'

'I – er – I just wondered.'

He was obviously telling the truth. He was carrying an atlas and some drawing things. One or two other boys, similarly equipped, strolled past them as they talked.

'Going to be a fine night,' said Fearless affably.

'Er – yes.'

'I say, are you all right?'

'Perfectly, thank you,' said Josephine with dignity, while, in fact, feeling foolish.

She considered mentioning the occupant of the upstairs room to Matron, in a casual sort of way, but for the rest of that day she could not get herself into the mood to be casual. The following afternoon, when she went into Matron's room, she was distracted from this intention. Matron was sitting at her table on which was spread a beautiful tea-set: six plates, cups and saucers, slop basin, milk jug, teapot, with a pattern of gold, red and blue.

'Oh! Lovely!'

Matron nodded. 'Crown Derby.'

'From – ?'

Matron nodded. 'He doesn't want to drink tea out of flower pots any more.'

'But that's good!'

'Yes,' said Matron; but she looked rather numb. She began packing the exquisite china back in its straw. Josephine watched her uncertainly.

'Jo,' said Matron, 'do you think this is a good joke? "Why does Smith call his motor-car Fishy? Because he has to kipper look out that it doesn't bloater pieces."'

'Not very,' said Josephine, shuddering slightly.

'Neither do I. I don't like to discourage him, because he is trying so hard, and I'd like him back really, but I don't think I could stand up to that sort of thing for long.'

'Oh dear,' said Josephine.

CHAPTER THIRTEEN

Trubbs Minor taught Yo-Yo to three age-groups for an hour each twice a week. The school was now supplying a stock of practice Yo-Yos, cheap and rather crude, but suitable for rough handling by beginners. These encouraged Trubbs to try out daring new moves. One he called 'conkers'. This involved simply cracking your opponent's Yo-Yo with your own, conker fashion, but it was performed according to etiquette as strict as *hara-kiri*, the ceremonial suicide of Japan. You faced your opponent at a distance of one yard and were not allowed to move your feet on pain of disqualification. Both Yo-Yos had to descend fully and rise again twice before contact was allowed, the strike being effected on the third descent. The skill lay in bluffing your opponent to go first for that third descent, and then dropping upon him from above. It required a cool head and steady nerves, and Trubbs preached to his followers that it came easiest to the pure in heart. It caused much accidental cracking of fingers and Matron was kept busy with sticking plaster. It added competitive zest to the pure art of Yo-Yo, and Trubbs hoped to include it in contests with other schools.

Trubbs was thinner, and really did seem taller, until you saw him beside his fellow Fourth Formers, who dwarfed him. The illusion was caused by his tilting his head slightly backwards, loftily, as if in disdain of common humanity. This brought his school tie into prominence, and gave him a commanding air which compensated for his lack of inches, making taller boys look down sheepishly when he faced them. But sometimes he looked tired, for his new responsibility was a strain.

Josephine went to watch his classes quite often. One afternoon, when the boys had gone and she was congratulating him on their progress, he coughed and looked at his feet, then looked resolutely up and said: 'Tugnutt.'

'Mm?' (She had noticed for some while that his voice had changed. She had supposed that it was breaking, a phenomenon new in her experience, whereby a boy's tones would plunge and zoom in a manner to outdo the Yo-Yo itself. But it was not breaking, it was just charged with a new, imperious note of authority.)

'Tugnutt, I have something serious to say to you.'

'Go on, then.'

'I want us to break off our engagement.'

'Yes, all right.'

'You see, I – I have so much on my plate just now', said Trubbs awkwardly, 'that it really isn't fair to you to hold you to it.'

'No, all right.'

'I'm doing this for your sake, Tugnutt.'

'Yes, of course.'

'I want to do the decent thing.'

'Very considerate.'

'Jolly good of you to take it so well, Tugnutt.'

Josephine shook hands with him gravely, and walked back to her room smiling. There was a lesson here, though. That 'I'm doing it for your sake' had a male ring to it, and she should be prepared to hear it again some time in her life. Her tablets: meet it was she set it down.

By night she lay uneasily in her bed. It made her most uncomfortable to think that there might be a Thing overhead. It could not have been Fearless; Fearless had been accounted for. Suddenly she remembered Cardew. Oh, what a relief! Yes, the cad Cardew was in cahoots with Fearless! And he had a slinky way of moving about that accorded well with the smooth sounds she had heard in that room. Cardew! Oh, good!

But what was he up to? Never mind; she had no fear of Cardew.

Reassured, she slept soundly. The next day she checked up whether the Remove had had a private study period at the time she had heard the sounds. Yes, they had.

Yet her fears crept back, not to be denied. There was no proof that it had been Cardew . . . Mr Victor and his smouldering eyes had had a profound effect on her, a fact that she could not help betraying to Porson, who felt uneasy and insecure when she was worried and crossly expostulated with her.

'Look,' he said, 'if you believe what I think you believe, well, all I can say is . . . I mean, you're brainy, you're much brainer than I am, but when it comes to Victor and his ridiculous experiments you're like some baby.'

'I know,' said Josephine humbly. This was good sense. Her father and brothers would have said much the same.

'Pity Victor nearly killed himself,' said Porson, softening. 'He might have explained all this bilge. What about that formula?'

'There was nothing in the lab.'

'Shall I help you look again?'

'There's no point.'

'Worth a try?'

'No. Oh well, all right.'

It was evening, and quite dark. They had been pacing up and down a path behind the gym (they were squeamish nowadays about meeting in the woods) and now they went through an old routine. Josephine went to her room and sat in darkness, and some minutes later Porson slipped in through the open window. From there, as stealthily as though exposed to snipers, they crept up to the bio lab.

Josephine had not told Porson about the sounds from the floor above, because he was a conscientious House Captain and a born worrier. She felt apprehensive. Suppose it had not been Cardew after all, and the alien overhead chose this moment to return to its sand box, as human beings (so psychology assures us) sometimes desire to return to the womb? No, that was too fanciful; and here was the sturdy Porson peering about with his torch. She loved him at this moment.

A thorough examination of drawers and cupboards, and even the space behind the blackboard on the wall, disclosed nothing. In the inner room, as before, they were able to switch on the light, but still their search was in vain.

'Well,' said Josephine, 'as I told you – '

'What about his coat?'

'Now why didn't I think of that?'

Porson took the white coat from its hook and felt in all the pockets.

'Here's something.'

It was a sheet of paper from a writing pad. They spread it out on the seat of a chair. It was covered with arcane hieroglyphics.

'Does this mean anything to you?'

Josephine shook her head.

'I suppose this is the key to that Ray of his.'

'Maybe. I was just wondering if you had to join all these squiggles up with a pencil and make a face.'

'Victor ought to be jolly grateful to you.'

'And to you.'

They were pleased with each other, and went out with their arms round each other, and kissed at the door of the bio lab, before crawling like gunpowder plotters down the stairs again.

'He's quite comfortable, but I wouldn't call him sensible,' said Sister. 'He's like a parrot. He says the same thing over and over again.' A good professional, she almost concealed her impatience with Mr Victor, but not quite. '"Formula" is his favourite word. After that it's "Tugnutt".'

'I'm flattered.'

'Whisht, and you can't be hard up for flatterers,' said Sister, smiling.

'The formula – I think I've found it.'

'Well, glory be to God. Let's hope it makes him happy.'

'Perhaps we should break it to him gently?'

But Sister had changed her views on taxing Mr Victor. 'Oh, come on,' she said briskly. 'Kill or cure, eh?'

She led Josephine into the private ward where Mr Victor was sitting up in bed, silent and misunderstood.

He grabbed the formula as a traveller in the Sahara might a drink of water and for some moments sat gobbling over it. Then he looked up with so aggrieved an expression that he seemed about to burst into tears.

'Why have you taken so long?'

'I couldn't find it, sir. It was in your coat.'

'Well, of course it was.'

'Sir,' said Josephine, 'is this – ?'

'Is it what? Never mind, never mind. Can't explain now.'

'You've found your tongue, anyway,' said Sister tartly.

Mr Victor, still mummified by bandages, alarmed them by swinging his legs out of bed, standing up for a second, and pitching over to sprawl across his bed again.

'Steady!' exclaimed Sister angrily. 'What on earth do you think you're – '

Mr Victor stood up again and wobbled a few steps, much as Josephine had imagined his monster would in its first moments of creation. He lurched into Sister, who bore him back to his bed with strong arms.

'Holy Mary!' In her temper, her Irish accent was more pronounced. 'What in the name of God are you up to? Now you stay there, hear me?'

'It is essential – '

'It's essential that you stay in that bed or I'll tie you down, so I will.'

Mr Victor dropped back on his pillows, moaning. 'Oh, my God! Beleaguered by fools!'

'Sir, is there anything I can do?' asked Josephine mildly.

'Get out!' Mr Victor began sobbing wildly. 'Get out, get out!'

'Sure, and it'll be a pleasure,' said Sister grimly, 'after you've had a sedative.'

She joined Josephine in the corridor a few minutes later.

'Well, like I said, kill or cure. Kill, if he carries on like that.'

'Grateful, wasn't he?'

'All men are the same, darling.'
'Yes, they might be.'

She had gone alone to the hospital this time. When she
went through the Main Gate she came upon Mr Mundy
sitting on his favourite bench and looking pensive. She
could not avoid him and her heart sank. She dreaded
being told a joke, for to be forced to laugh at unfunny
jokes is one of the most depressing experiences on
earth.

Mr Mundy being Mr Mundy, no matter what theory
held him in thrall, Josephine had often marvelled that
the nice Matron had ever married him. Perhaps she felt
protective to Mr Mundy's boringness. Yes, that was it.
We do shrink from hurting the feelings of bores. Matron
must have this feeling very highly developed, though.

Josephine waved and called gaily, 'Good afternoon!'
and made to stride on, but he stopped her with an
outstretched hand, like a traffic policeman.

'As you shut the gate on one neurosis another knocks
at the door,' he said.

Josephine resigned herself to sitting beside him.

'I've explained to you about the Woodcutter
Complex?'

'I seem to remember you did, Mr Mundy, yes.'

'I can't expect you to understand, but your innocence
stimulates me. I am overcoming the Woodcutter Complex. I read the *Daily Telegraph*. I buy expensive china. I
make jokes.'

'That's good, isn't it?'

'No. My wit is not appreciated. My wife only pre-
tends to laugh, and my colleagues merely look glum.'

Josephine's encounter with Mr Victor had knocked
the stuffing out of her but she braced herself, drew her
fur close round her neck, looked like a girl on a

chocolate box and said in her best out-of-the-mouths-of-babes voice: 'I – I wonder if your humour is too subtle for them, Mr Mundy?'

'Ah,' said Mr Mundy indulgently. He was pleased. 'What would you do about that?'

'Perhaps. . .Perhaps you should tell the jokes to yourself and sort of laugh inwardly.'

'You're a funny child.'

Funnier than you, anyway, thought Josephine. 'Excuse me, I really must go to a lesson.'

She went off at a little run to her imaginary lesson. Mr Mundy sat chuckling at her *naïveté*. He'd bitten, though. Laugh inwardly? She pictured a kettle coming to the boil.

She had by now a longing for nothing but her own company, but as luck would have it she met Trubbs Minor in the Quad. He was carrying a copy of *Yo-Yo News*, a cyclostyled quarterly, and he stopped her, looking concerned.

'Tugnutt, it says here that there's a chap in Japan who can work four Yo-Yos at once.'

'How does he do that?'

'One in each hand and one from each foot.'

'Well, never mind.'

But he did mind. Josephine had not anticipated that his success would bring its own worries along with it.

'He sits on top of a step-ladder, it says,' said Trubbs fretfully. 'I could do that, I suppose. Do you think I could work one from my mouth as well? That would make it five.'

Josephine knew that her answers to these successive appeals for help were becoming rather specious, but she was weary and needed rest. Still, she had a responsibility to Trubbs. She drew a deep breath. 'No,' she said.

'Someone will make it seven by working one from each ear. What you've got to do is invent a new kind of Yo-Yo. The round ones have become too commonplace. What about one shaped like a violin? Or a pig – yes, one like a pig that squeals "God Save the King". That's a *very* nice idea.'

She patted the Captain of Yo-Yo on the head and went on, leaving him standing there open-mouthed and the cult of the Yo-Yo just about to enter the first phase of its decadence.

CHAPTER FOURTEEN

Every day, Mr Cropper crept to the Poste Restante counter at the Post Office to see if there was anything for him from *Woman's Star*. He nursed a pathetic (and widely held) belief that the longer an editor kept a manuscript, the better its chances of acceptance, and as 'The Fragrant Altar' had been away for nearly three weeks he could not suppress a weak flutter of hope. He told himself stoutly, as a corrective, that he must expect rejection, repeated rejection; this was a mill through which every writer had to go. But no writer ever sends in a manuscript in the absolute certainty that it will be returned, and so Mr Cropper's weak flutter persisted.

Every time he went to the Poste Restante counter he had a faint-hearted wish that there woul be nothing for him. It reprieved him for another twenty-four hours and added one more day of shaky hope. If there was something for him it would be either a small thin envelope or a long fat one, the one causing joy, the other, reason though he might, a sinking of the heart.

This afternoon there was, indeed, something for him, and it was, indeed, a long fat envelope, self-addressed. He said, 'Thank you,' quietly to the clerk and went to a corner of the Post Office to open it. Mild resentment mingled with his disappointment. He said to himself what every rejected writer has always said, and with perfect reason, that his story was at least as good as some that he had seen in print; but in the few steps that it took to reach the corner his natural humility had returned and he was questioning his presumption in supposing that he would ever be worth printing at all.

He slit the envelope open with a small mother-of-pearl-handled knife, in his neat way, and drew out the contents. Here it was, his manuscript, with the paper clip slightly dislodged. He glanced at it with intense dislike and put it back. But what was this? Not a rejection-slip, but a small white envelope with 'Woman's Star' printed on the top left-hand corner. He slit this open too, expecting no more than the Editor's regrets discreetly sheathed; but it contained a letter, which he unfolded with strange stirrings in his breast.

Dear Miss Greaves,

I have read your story, 'The Fragrant Altar', with interest, and in several ways it looked like a good story to me. You have a talent for narrative and can convey powerful emotion, and but for one objection, I would have accepted it for publication without hesitation.

That objection was the difference in ages between the two principal characters. As a general rule we like the hero to be some years older than the heroine, but I feel that a gap of forty-three years is really rather excessive, and most of our younger readers might find it difficult to believe in.

I wonder if you could see your way to making your heroine perhaps a little older than seventeen and your hero younger than sixty? I realize that this would involve a radical rewriting, but if you were willing to undertake it I would be glad to give your story further consideration.

Yours sincerely, Marjorie Clarke, Fiction Editor.

'Stupid of me,' said Mr Cropper to himself, 'unforgiveably stupid. I'm a fool.'

Never mind. As the significance of the letter sank in, he stood there flushed and shaking so much that for some minutes he could not move. He read the letter through twice more, then went back with it to his room where he read it another twenty-nine times.

'Oh, Mr Cropper,' said Josephine, 'you're a success!'

'Come, come, Miss Tugnutt, I may not succeed in rewriting it to the Editor's satisfaction.'

'Yes, you will, of course you will.'

'Then you must advise me. My heroine shall be – how old?'

Josephine thought of a good mature age. 'Nineteen or twenty.'

'And the hero – thirty-five?'

'With dark hair greying slightly at the temples.'

'Yes, of course. How foolish I've been, Miss Tugnutt.'

'You've been wonderful, with your very first attempt!'

'That is indeed very gratifying,' said Mr Cropper gently, 'but I have still been foolish.'

Then, for she showed a flicker of embarrassment, he added stoutly, 'I shall set to work at my earliest opportunity. I think it is very good of the Editor to afford me this latitude. But as for you, my dear, I can never repay you for what you have done for me.'

A grateful client at last, thought Josephine, as she crossed the Quad. I always thought he was the best of the lot.

She had not read Mr Cropper's story, but she had learned something of it from the Editor's letter, and what it taught her had her near tears. At the same time she wanted to turn cartwheels across the Quad. She could have done so, too, easily; but of course her sense of decorum prevented her.

'I was told he was terribly violent,' said Josephine to Matron as they took tea together, 'but when you get to know him properly, he's as gentle as a lamb.'

'Yes, often it's the other way round,' said Matron.

A day or two later, Mr Victor discharged himself from the hospital, to the mixed relief and indignation of the nursing staff. He re-entered St Chauvin's to almost no notice. The masters said, 'Oh, hello, Victor. Better now? Good. Just what *was* the trouble?' and walked away before he could answer; and the boys were hardly aware that he had returned at all. He spent much of his time limping, with a sort of savagery in his limp, about the town, and the rest of it in the inner room in his lab. Josephine had expected him to run through his repertoire of brooding postures over the sand box, muttering, 'What went wrong? Just *what* went wrong?' but he paid it no attention. He kept producing the formula and studying it as if it were a watch and he was running out of time. He ignored Josephine completely.

'Well, ignore him back,' said Porson.

'I do, don't worry. I don't even go to his lessons. I just use the lab when I want to.'

Yet she could not help feeling that Mr Victor stood as a loose end, an unsolved case in her book. The term was nearing its end, and with it her stay at St Chauvin's, and her other cases were resolved. (Were they 'her cases'? If so, they'd been thrust upon her, hadn't they?) Mr Cropper? Yes, she was joyful about him, foreseeing him becoming a number of household names that she kept making up for him: Penelope Waynefleet, for one, and perhaps Charmian Moone, Phillida Grayle and even Andromeda Starr. Trubbs Minor? A triumph, although she could not help feeling that, after all, she had liked him better as a Weed.

119

Mr Mundy? The fact was that Matron had given in her notice and would be leaving at the end of term to resume married life with him. Well, as long as he bought her expensive tea-sets and kept off the jokes, Josephine couldn't see why it shouldn't work. So far he was indeed keeping off the jokes.

'He's acquired one peculiar habit, mind,' said Matron. 'He has a way of going red in the face as if he were holding his breath, and hissing a little. Still, I can put up with that.'

'He seems to be trying hard,' said Josephine.

So far so good, then.

But Mr Victor: well, he had never been a 'case' like the others – she'd never offered him advice – but simply to fill a box with sand and then blow it to pieces did seem a tame conclusion to his grandiose project, and Josephine felt vaguely cheated and even ventured to hope that with his precious formula restored to him he might bring off a sensation yet. But the term was running out, and she didn't think she'd be around to see it.

There was something else. A new *frisson* was going round St Chauvin's.

Tugnutt fever had all but died by now. St Chauvin's was taking Josephine for granted. Her sinister influence was a fading memory and soon she herself would also disappear. When revolution seems imminent the strength of the establishment shows itself. She was content for St Chauvin's to become a fading memory too. She'd plucked the best from it: she had Porson.

Yes, he was the best, and she did love him. He seemed the epitome of St Chauvin's conformity and yet he was quite different from the rest. The good soldier will march over a cliff if not ordered to halt. His not to reason why. Yet, as he falls through the air, he may well acknowledge to himself that someone has blundered. Porson was like that soldier. He knew what St Chauvin's was like. It was not in his power to change it, nor his duty to try. He had the old feudal virtue of loyalty. When the chance came he would be loyal to higher things. She loved him.

But Porson was worried on account of the *frisson*, and Josephine was disturbed because it prevented her from swanning through the last few days of term, doing nothing but day-dream about meeting him in the holidays.

The *frisson* first made itself felt, surprisingly enough, not at St Chauvin's but in Woebegone Abbey, to the marvellously attuned senses of Fanshawe-Smith, alias Brother Bartholomew.

He had been getting less and less contented with Woebegone Abbey as a haven. Looking over the wall, he saw farm girls working in the fields and he was sure that they were closing in on the Abbey, like Red Indians on a stockade, and would in due course spring. Sometimes these girls showed their low cunning by turning their backs and working further away. Sensing, with his acute instinct, that Tugnutt fever had subsided in the school, and that by next term Josephine would have gone without trace, he decided to resign from the monastery and rejoin the Classical Sixth where he would be in an even more enclosed order than he was at present.

But just as he was on his way to the Abbot's room, with the words 'Reverend Father, I am no longer a monk' forming on his lips, he was arrested by a terrible premonition. Something was going on at St Chauvin's, and it had something to do with Tugnutt.

'The Whore of Babylon is abroad there,' he muttered.

Of course, you have to make allowances for his choice of terms. But he was right: in St Chauvin's, as in the arbour, something stirred, and it was not mice.

Fanshawe-Smith turned and hurried out into the open. He looked so sick that Brother Francis, noticing him, asked him sympathetically whether he had stomach-ache.

The rest of the school, not being psychic like Fanshawe-Smith, could not put a name to the *frisson* but felt it deeply. It was all the worse for being nameless. Emotional boys took to having fist fights with their best friends. Stolid boys fainted in morning assembly. A group of juniors at practice with Trubbs flung down their Yo-Yos and ran out in tears. Questioned, they could not say what had come over them. They were in a worse state even than when Josephine had first entered the school because at least she had been a visible influence; this was uncanny.

Was it, she could not help wondering, some sort of after-effect of Mr Victor's explosion? She knew this was probably sheer superstition and did not dare mention it to Porson. Nevertheless the notion of a Thing on the topmost floor came back, and would not go away.

Porson was baffled, because one cannot go looking for an atmosphere, and his frustration made him bad-tempered. 'What atmosphere?' he would snap. 'You're always imagining things.' Then he would repent and make overtures to her. She did not enjoy this state of things. Not long ago they had been happy and friendly, and it had been sweet, and she wanted that mood back.

So much did she want it back that she did something very brave. She left her room in the darkness of a December afternoon and went up to the top floor in search of she knew not what.

On the previous occasion she had moved very quietly. This time – for she was very nervous – she switched on all the lights in the corridor and coughed and stamped her feet as if to frighten away evil spirits. The evil spirits, if any were there, took the hint: there were no sounds from that left-side room.

No, the corridor was deserted. The only sound was of rain pattering against the long windows at the end. Josephine walked towards them. Her reflection in the glass looked back at her. So, for about one second, did the reflection of someone else.

It was a young woman, olive-skinned, sloe-eyed, with a yard of snaky black hair.

A door shut with the softest of clicks and the reflection vanished.

CHAPTER FIFTEEN

In the dark of the glass, with rain streaming about her, the girl, reflected, had a savage unearthly look. Josephine's first reaction was that Mr Victor's experiment had worked and had brought forth not a man but an earth-mother: Lillith instead of Adam. Then she moved with a kind of fury akin to panic; she ran along the corridor hammering on doors and shouting, 'Who's there?' and, 'Come out!' and, 'It's no use your hiding,' and so on; and then she scuttled down the stone stairs so fast that her feet made a noise like a stick being dragged along railings.

She paused for a fraction in the doorway on to the Lower Quad and then made a dash through the rain. She must find Porson. Wherever in this labyrinthine madhouse was Porson? Not in the Main Quad. Oh, why wasn't he *there* when she wanted him? She looked in at the entrance hall of the Main Building. Oh, there he was, calmly pinning something to the notice board! He was taken aback by her onslaught and wasted minutes by answering foolishly: 'Where? Who is? But who is she?' and so on, till Josephine all but pounded him with her fists.

'Have you got the keys to the top floor?' she demanded.

'No. The Housemaster will have some. I could ask him for them, but he'll want to know what for – '

'Oh, you might as well send for them through the post! We'll have to do without them. She's probably miles away by now, but – Oh, do come on!'

Porson came on, hurriedly but reluctantly, because he distrusted female fears and at the same time had a horrid feeling that they might be justified; but by the time they reached the top corridor the girl, if she was not just lying low, had slipped away.

'Sure you didn't imagine it?'

'I no more imagined it than we imagined that noise in the wood.'

'Well, there must have been a perfectly normal explanation for that –'

'There's a perfectly normal explanation for this, too. I saw a girl reflected in the window. I didn't say I saw a ghost. She must have looked out of one of these rooms to see who I was, spotted that I could see her in the window, and dived back. I heard the door shut.'

'But what was a *girl* doing up here?'

'Oh, really, what a good question!'

But now he looked so baffled and downcast that she took pity on him.

'Oh, I'm sorry! It's not your fault!'

'I could ask Mr Johnson to organize a proper search, I suppose,' muttered Porson, 'but –'

The 'but' was heavy. But what had they been up to on a disused floor that was out of bounds?

'No, don't.'

'There's been something in the air ever since that explosion,' said Porson heavily.

This was the opposite of what he usually said but Josephine only hastened to reassure him.

'No, don't you get like that. You're the only sane person here, and I don't want you to change.'

'Even so –'

'Never mind "even so". This'll settle itself somehow. Let's forget about it.'

'It's hard to make you out, sometimes.'

'I know. I shouldn't have dragged you up here. I'm sorry I panicked.'

They were friends again. But 'forget about it'? The best he could hope for was that the term would end and force her to. They went downstairs.

On the floor below they had to pass the bio lab. In their relief at leaving the top floor they were incautious in their movements, and almost collided with Mr Victor as he hurried into it. It didn't matter; he did not see them. He wouldn't have noticed a troop of guards. His eyes were wild. He muttered to himself.

Why didn't Josephine tell Porson her suspicion that Fearless, and perhaps Cardew as well, had been up to that top corridor? Yes, that is a fair question. Perhaps she was afraid of committing the unforgivable sin of sneaking. Perhaps it was due to some odd reluctance of her own.

But she saw no objection to confronting Fearless himself.

She was still on polite terms with him. He knew what she knew about him, and she knew that he knew, but nothing had been said. So she approached him with what seemed guileless friendliness, and said: 'You know the school awfully well, Fearless. Can you explain something to me?'

'If I can,' he answered, smiling.

'What was a strange girl doing on the top floor of the Old Building?'

'A *girl*?'

'A girl.'

'Might be some fellow's sister?'

'Yes, I myself am some fellow's sister but that doesn't explain why she was there. You're not suggesting that she got left over from Open Day?'

This was good, sarcastic stuff but all it did was give him time to think.

'Could it have been the new Matron?'

'I doubt it very much. Why should she be up there?'

'Maybe some new French *assistante*?'

'Fearless, you know that this school doesn't go in for female French *assistantes*, and anyway, why should she be – '

'Lost her way, perhaps?'

'Oh, *really* – '

'I'm afraid I've run out of ideas,' said Fearless, still bland, still smiling. 'I'm so sorry I can't be more helpful, Tugnutt. And now if you'll excuse me, I must go to maths.'

He had won that round all right. All she had done was to alert him.

He *was* alerted, though. His smile looked just a little fixed, his easy manner was just a little too easy to be natural. Cardew looked strained, too. With good strategy, Fearless never let Josephine see himself with Cardew, but the cad of the Remove now wore, she was sure, a shiftier look than before. It was hard to tell because Cardew's glances had always been sidelong, but now they were more sidelong than ever.

Oh, well, said Josephine to herself, only a few days left anyway. Let sleeping dogs lie.

But the sleeping dogs were aroused. The atmosphere in the school became more highly charged than ever. Like the pattering feet and panting breath of the Dorset Wolf in the woods, a presence was making itself felt.

Mr Johnson, sheltering in his room, was at a loss to know what to do. He simply hoped against hope that the crisis would spend itself, just as Tugnutt fever had died away.

Or had it? Strange things had happened since that girl came. You couldn't attribute them directly to her, but . . .

Mr Johnson feared the female sex just as much as did Fanshawe-Smith, and if he had been as honest as the latter he might well have become a monk himself. As it was, he had chosen to pretend that women didn't exist. But now, as on some Sabbath of witches, a sinister spirit was abroad. Mr Johnson read and reread his favourite passages in *Scouting for Boys*, but this time the good words did not comfort him.

There was a knock at the door and Mr Cropper came in.

Mr Cropper's recovery had been one of those strange things of this term; indeed, it had been a miracle. Somehow, he had found inner peace. He was happy.

But now he did not look happy nor inwardly peaceful at all. He sank into a chair, looking as if he had awakened from day-dreams to a dreadful night. Finally he said, 'I'm afraid I'm going to have to turn teaching in, Johnson.'

'Really? Why?'

'I think my mind is going again.'

'Whatever makes you think that?' asked Mr Johnson, touched.

'I used to be mad, as you well know. I'm going mad again. I'm having hallucinations.'

'What sort of hallucinations?' demanded Mr Johnson, alerted.

'I thought I saw a young woman.'

Mr Johnson rose slowly to his feet as if hoisted by an invisible crane.

'A young . . . ? Tugnutt?'

'No, no, not Miss Tugnutt. A strange young woman. By the garages next to the Old Building. I blinked, and she disappeared.'

'Disappeared?'

'Yes. At first I thought that young Fearless of the Fifth dashed up and shoved her into a garage, but when I asked him, "Where did that girl go?" he replied with the greatest astonishment, "What girl, sir?"'

'Fearless.'

'Yes. A decent young fellow.'

'Yes.'

'I can only conclude that I had an hallucination, and it's time for me to resign. I may pursue a literary career,' said Mr Cropper, rambling on. 'I'm having some modest success in that field, and – '

'Wait a bit,' interrupted Mr Johnson. 'Don't be too hasty. This may not have been an hallucination. No, no one has seen anything, to my knowledge, but there's undoubtedly a *spirit* abroad in this school, and – '

'Really? A spirit?'

'I'm surprised you haven't noticed it.'

Mr Cropper's unwordly face lit up. 'A spirit! So I saw some sort of simulacrum, did I? After all, the school's old, isn't it? She's some sort of bally ghost, what? You've no idea how relieved I am. I'm awfully glad I spoke to you, Johnson. What a load off my mind!'

When he had gone, Mr Johnson sat hunched and brooding for some minutes. Then he went to the Headmaster, coughed several times, went red and stammered: 'I don't quite know how to put this, Headmaster. There's – there's an atmosphere – a kind of spirit – abroad in the school – '

'There is indeed, Johnson. An *esprit de corps*. One is proud of it.'

'No . . . ' Mr Johnson gathered his forces again, and tried another tack. 'Er – Cropper says he saw a girl – '

'That would be my niece, Joanna Tugwell.'

'No, sir. A – a strange girl.'

The Headmaster gave a booming laugh. 'So Cropper saw a girl! Ha ha! Our Thespians have taken him in!'

'I beg your pardon, sir?'

'One of the Dramatic Society boys dressed up for the school play, my dear fellow! What Shakespeare's actors could do, St Chauvin's men can emulate, eh?'

'Really, Headmaster, Cropper did give me the impression – '

An owl in sunlight could not have been more inscrutably bland than the Headmaster at this moment.

'Johnson,' he said, in a voice of gentle but infinite reproach, 'we of St Chauvin's are not interested in scandal. In a school of our standing, what other explanation than mine could there be?'

'So we need not worry,' said Mr Johnson, defeated.

'Not at all. Tell Cropper that pretty soon he'll see this "girl" shoving in the scrum!'

' "Shoving in the scrum!" ' repeated Mr Johnson, back in his own room. He began giggling and clutching at his hair. 'Young lady, you are (a) some sort of bally ghost (b) a boy dressed up . . . and I claim the ten pounds reward . . . If Fearless of the Fifth doesn't get there first . . . '

He controlled himself. 'Fearless,' he said soberly.

Fearless was excellent in a crisis. He had shown impressive presence of mind several times this term. The other boys looked up to him. He might be just the man to handle this situation.

'Imagination, sir,' said Fearless.

'I'd like to think so, Fearless, but there's some evidence. Mr Cropper – '

'Mr Cropper saw nothing, sir. I was there.'

'But how did this . . . *atmosphere* come about?'

Fearless wavered and shrugged. 'Atmospheres just do, sir. It was the Dorset Wolf not long ago.'

'So it was.' But Mr Johnson, looking keenly at Fearless, saw that he looked pale.

'A bit off colour, Fearless?'

'Actually, sir, yes, I am.'

'Why is that?'

'It's – it's awfully hard to find a way of putting this, sir . . . I'm afraid you'll think it awful cheek, sir – '

'Go on.'

'I – I – ' Fearless seemed to summon his courage, and blurted out, 'I don't think it was a frightfully good idea to have let a girl into the school in the first place, sir.'

'I take it you mean the Headmaster's niece?'

'Well, yes, sir. I know it isn't any of my dashed business, sir. And she's Fitted In jolly well, sir. I'm not saying anything against her, sir. But – '

'Go on, Fearless.'

'It's just that – it's just that somehow she – creates an atmosphere just by being here, sir. She's – well, she's not One of Us, is she, sir?'

'I know exactly what you mean, Fearless.'

'I'm jolly glad, sir, because it was jolly difficult to say.'

'Yes, I understand. And you really think that's the reason?'

'I don't see what else it could be, sir.'

'I hope you're right. And I think you well may be. Well, she leaves us in just one week.'

'Well, no disrespect, sir, but I'll be glad. We – we don't need any feminine influence here, sir.'

'Between ourselves, Fearless, I heartily agree with you. I'm glad we've had this little chat.'

Fearless went off looking like a mourner at a funeral. When he gained the Quad he looked up and winked at the stars. Mr Johnson lit his pipe and was comforted. A sound fellow, Fearless.

Josephine knew nothing of all this, of course, but she had already noticed a certain pallor of face and uneasiness of manner in Fearless. Whatever he was up to seemed to be getting him down. Perhaps Fate was catching up with him. She had always believed that it would.

Or – was it that this atmosphere in the school, which was now like a miasma, was nothing to do with Fearless but something quite separate, something that he couldn't explain, which was disturbing his plans?

Being female herself, Josephine thought the Mystery of Woman to be largely a myth. Even if there were a girl roving about the top corridor like the mad woman in *Jane Eyre*, she did not believe that that alone could cause this weird malaise. There was something else.

That explosion of Mr Victor's had had a delayed reaction and sent a sort of shock wave through the school. He was *not* to be written off. They hadn't heard the last of him yet.

Meanwhile he laboured away in his lab, joining wires and peering cross-eyed at them, and uttering occasional staccato exclamations.

CHAPTER SIXTEEN

'Well, Jo,' said Matron, 'in three days' time I'll be shaking the dust of St Chauvin's off my feet! I hope I'm doing the right thing.'

'But it's what you want, Matron, isn't it?'

'Is it what he wants, too? He worries me. Yes, he's, well, *reformed* – but he has this way of going all red in the face – purple – and he seems to be boiling inside. I hope I'm not making him go against his nature.'

Josephine started. These words had a familiar ring.

'Well,' she said uncertainly, 'if you like him better as he is now – '

'I'm not sure that I do. I don't want him pretending all the time.'

'It's my wife,' Josephine heard Mr Mundy saying. *'She's forced an alien personality on me . . . it's her unconscious desires at work . . .'*

Good Heavens. Matron on the one hand, reasonable and long suffering; her husband on the other, daft and insufferable – and yet, when you looked at it again, how could you tell just who was doing what to whom in this marriage? Josephine was shaken.

Mr Victor, she discovered, was now working late into the night, perhaps all night long. She could see the reflection of light from the bio lab on the stairs when she went to her room at bedtime. What he was up to was beyond guessing, but it was consuming him mentally and physically. He was a gaunt, wild figure, doing, apparently, without either food or sleep, and it was as well that he had no teaching to do for he would have had no strength left for it.

More than once she came close to asking him what he was about, and she still believed that he wanted her to, but their perverse battle of wills went on and she refrained. She felt protective towards Mr Victor and he clearly needed protecting. But her confidence in her management of other people's lives was not quite as strong as it once had been, and she left him alone for the time being.

After lunch, her last here but two, she came out into the Lower Quad, and being much exercised in her mind, leaned for a moment against the door of the nearest garage. The Quad sulked in dull yellow December light, so fitting to the atmosphere of the school that she wondered whether it was different in the world outside.

Her weight on the garage door made it shut with a soft click. It had been very slightly ajar. She opened it and looked inside. The garage was empty. In the left-hand wall was a door which she opened to find herself in a disused scullery with a pitted floor and a much crazed sink, with taps greenish and corroded. This little room led out to the back of the stairs, so that one could discreetly enter the Old Building without having to walk the length of the corridor from the main entrance.

There was a third door at the other end of the garage. She tried it: it too was unlocked. It opened on to fields and a footpath that went down to the town.

Her first thought was that Trubbs Minor had had no need to try to climb to the roof of this garage, but could have walked right through it and quite altered his subsequent career. Her next thought was mildly erotic: this garage led to an excellent spot for a meeting with Porson.

She picked her way along the backs of the garages to a corner overhung by a tree. Yes, a secluded spot. She made to return, then stopped and shrank back. She thought she heard footsteps in the garage from which she had come. Sure enough, the door opened a moment later and a woman emerged and set off down the path.

Yes, it was the one whose reflection she had seen. She was much older than she had looked in the dark of the window: in her mid-thirties, perhaps. She was slim and shapely, with a mane of black hair over the back of her white raincoat. She was olive-complexioned, good-looking, and hard-eyed.

Josephine waited until she was out of sight, and then went straight to the top floor of the Old Building and tried the door of the room from which she had heard the sounds. It was unlocked. She went in, though it took all her courage. It was like looking into Mr Victor's sand box.

And it was just as much of an anticlimax. What she had expected she did not know, but it had been vaguely horrible. What she saw was a desk with a folder on it, a waste-paper basket and a chair.

She sat down at the desk and opened the folder. It contained a sheet of foolscap paper drawn up in columns. In the left-hand column was a list of names inked in in block capitals.

Adamson. Bannington Major. Brownlow. Culham. Digby. Ewing ... They were senior boys at St Chauvin's.

In the next column there were some sparse statistics. 'Five feet ten inches. Slim. Likes dancing.' 'Five seven and a half. Fattish. Generally useless.' 'Five feet nine.

Stammers. V. frustrated – good risk.' Etc.

The third column was narrow and headed with two pound signs: ££. In this column there were stars: two for Adamson **, two for Bannington Major **, three for Culham ***. Digby got only one. And so on down the list. Josephine counted fifteen names in all.

The fourth and final column also contained names, lightly written in in pencil. Girls' names. Lulu. Maisie. Flo. Fifi. Francesca. Pearl. One or two had question marks after them, for example Maisie (?), who appeared to be paired with the fattish and generally useless Bannington Major.

Josephine sat over this list, puzzled and absorbed. Suddenly she felt that she was being watched, and she looked up to see Fearless of the Fifth in the doorway.

His face was grim. She stood up, taking her time. He really did seem set to attack her. Her brothers had shown her some judo moves, but she suspected that these worked only against strictly stylized attacks, preferably in slow motion. She decided that she would kick him on the shin and scream. There was no need: his face relaxed and he smiled. He was, incidentally, distinctly pale, but he smiled.

'Hello, Tugnutt,' he said easily. 'I'd just come to lock up.' He came in, closing the door. Josephine ran to it and put her back against it, gripping the doorknob behind her. Fearless smiled patiently and handed her the key. He strolled to the desk and sat down.

'I thought you'd catch up with me in the end,' he remarked. 'Lucky for me it is the end, almost. Only two days left, haven't you? There's not much you can do in that time.

'I don't underrate you, Tugnutt. I respect you, because we're two of a kind. Oh yes, we are, don't look so offended. We manipulate people, you and I. Isn't

136

that true? Isn't that what you do?

'Of course you could do the unforgivable and sneak on me, but you won't – it's not your style. And even if you did you wouldn't get anywhere. The Head wouldn't listen. He shuts his eyes to scandal. And Johnson – I'm sorry to say he doesn't like you very much, Tugnutt. He's afraid of you. I can't blame him.'

'Keep talking,' said Josephine.

'Thank you. It's a pleasure to talk to you. We'd have made a good team, but of course I ruled that out early. We don't see eye to eye.'

'I must say it's an honour to be classed with Cardew!'

'Oh, Cardew. He's an oaf. Shouldn't be mentioned in the same breath.'

Josephine's temper was rising. She felt she was losing ground.

'Fearless,' she demanded, 'who is that foreign-looking woman?'

'She's known in the trade as French Marie.'

'What trade?'

'She's in charge of a troupe of dancers in Cardew's father's night-club.'

'And those girls on the list are her dancers?'

'That's right. As a matter of fact,' said Fearless genially, 'you gave me the idea for this. You hadn't been at St Chauvin's more than a couple of days when I saw what a terrific effect a pretty girl was having on the school. I'd been cultivating Cardew for some while, you know, because there's a lot of money in night-clubs, and I like to be where the money is. But this gave me a direction.

'Well, you must have guessed what this is all about. French Marie and I are going to start up a dating agency. The senior boys have a great need for feminine company.'

'With Lulu and Fifi?'

'Certainly. They're as feminine as you can get.'

'Fearless,' said Josephine, breathing hard, 'if you're doing what I think you're doing –'

'Oh, come off it, Tugnutt. Why think the worst of everybody? I said it was a dating agency. What the boys get up to with their dates is no business of mine.'

'You'll never get away with it.'

'Oh, don't discourage me.'

'But is it worth the risk? St Chauvin's seniors don't get all that much pocket money, do they?'

'That's true,' said Fearless cheerfully, 'but their fathers do, you know. Have you noticed column three? The pound sign one with star ratings? The stars show how much wealth the paters possess. Rather as they grade hotels, you know. St Chauvin's paters are terrified of scandal.'

'You mean you intend to *blackmail* them?'

'Really, Tugnutt, you do use some ugly expressions.'

Beyond speech, Josephine stood for a while with her bosom heaving, like a heroine in the tales read by Mr Cropper.

'Well,' she said at last, 'I don't think you're as tough as you think you are. You've not been looking at all well lately. Your nerves are getting you down.'

'Yes,' said Fearless, and frowned. 'Yes, you're right, I am under the weather, but it's got nothing to do with my nerves. It's the atmosphere in this school. It's poisonous. I'd be all right myself, but French Marie is very sensitive to it. Every time she comes here she says it gives her the creeps.' Fearless's voice hardened. 'I don't want the thing to fizzle because she cracks up. You know something about the atmosphere, don't you, Tugnutt?'

'Do I?'

'Oh, come on. You're in league with Victor, aren't you?'

'Am I?'

'Look, I've been straight with you, now you be straight with me. I say you are in league with him, yes. Some funny things have happened this term. Old Cropper. Trubbs Minor. I imagine you've got at Matron, too, somehow. I know you're one hell of a girl, but I don't believe you could have done it all by yourself.'

'So what do you think I've been doing with Mr Victor?'

'You tell me.'

Josephine looked steadily at Fearless and saw that he was rattled. He was a cool customer, but for all his appearance of dark maturity he was still a schoolboy with some of the fears of childhood in him. Perhaps even the Dorset Wolf was among them.

'I'm not telling you anything,' she said.

Fearless went white. 'I don't want to lose my temper,' he said in a low and loaded voice. 'It's bad for me to lose my temper. But – '

Josephine, trembling inside, said quietly, 'Yes, it would be very bad for you to lose your temper with me. You might find that I had teeth.'

For a brief moment his eyes went wide with shock as the implications of this obscure remark made themselves felt, but he recovered quickly and became bland again.

'It doesn't matter. You've left it too late, Tugnutt. Two days left. One and a half – we pack up at noon on the last day. What could you do in that time?'

'What do you think?'

He was rattled again, but he controlled himself. 'Not enough to stop me, anyway.'

'Here's your key.'

'Oh, keep it if you like. I've got a duplicate.'

She put the key on the desk. 'Just one thing. Do these boys know about this?'

'Not yet. I've sounded them out, of course. Listed all the likely ones. But they don't know about the scheme.'

'So you could just tear this list up and forget the whole thing?'

'That would be a weak thing to do.'

'It'd be safe.'

'I'll call your bluff and chance it,' said Fearless, smiling.

CHAPTER SEVENTEEN

To have patched up a marriage, transmogrified a Weed, and brought purpose to the life of a good old man, all in the course of ten weeks was pretty good going for a budding psychiatrist, but all that was behind her now. Fearless's cool defiance rankled with Josephine. He was quite right that she wouldn't sneak on him, and quite right that even if she did he could easily outface her. He had a charmed life.

Oh, why should she bother anyway? It had nothing to do with her.

Yes, it had. There was Porson. He had another two terms to go before he left the school. This crazy scheme was bound to come out sooner or later, and if that happened in Porson's time the effect on him would be devastating. He was in charge of the House, and painfully conscientious. And everyone would let him take the blame.

Josephine went out into the Lower Quad and looked across to the Main Building, where, regardless of their doom, the little victims played.

She shook her head, defeated.

Fearless had done some hard thinking.

French Marie was due for a final visit to the school immediately after the last lesson this afternoon. He *must* put her off. She had been spotted twice now, by old Cropper and by Tugnutt, and although he'd handled each crisis very well, he dared not risk a third one. Tugnutt had rattled him yesterday afternoon more than he had let it show.

French Marie hated coming to the school anyway. She was a superstitious woman, and the oppressive atmosphere worried her. She came because her day was her own – she carried out her professional duties at night – whereas Fearless, who as a Fifth Former had no free periods, had to spend his day going to silly lessons. He would never play truant for fear of damaging his image.

He would phone her from the phone box outside the school at the earliest opportunity. Cancel the meeting. Hold everything till next term when Tugnutt would be out of the way and the whole place aired.

He sat through the last lesson chafing inwardly but outwardly bland. He even asked a few questions for the sake of appearances.

This proved to be unfortunate. The history master, a conscientious man, was worried lest his answers to this earnest pupil might have been rather superficial. He stopped Fearless on his way out from the lesson.

'Ah, Fearless: just spare me a moment. As to whether Elizabeth was really a good queen – well, opinions are divided on that subject! Let me just quote you a few. . .' He began fishing books from his shelves, and Fearless, with all the fortitude of the Spartan boy who let a fox eat away his vitals, stood there and suffered. The history master's 'moment' lasted ten minutes. Fearless may well have broken all school records in his final dash down the Main Drive. He flung himself panting into the telephone box.

A cleaner answered the phone.

'French Marie? Gawn.'

'Are you sure?'

'Tolja. Gawn.'

Damn, damn, damn, damn!

Only one thing for it. Wait in the field outside the garage and head French Marie off. He was not happy. He smelled disaster in the air.

On the afternoon of this penultimate day of the Christmas Term, Mr Cropper found a small, thin envelope waiting for him at the Poste Restante counter of the Post Office.

It contained no more than a slip of paper bearing 'the compliments of Concordant Press', with these words typed underneath: 'We like your revised version of "The Fragrant Altar", which we are publishing at our usual rates – Gladys Owen, for Marjorie Clarke, Fiction Ed., Woman's Star.'

Mr Cropper stood for a while suffused with joy, as if an angel had just assured him of everlasting bliss. Then he hastened back to the school, intent on sharing his good fortune with the nearest thing to an angel that he knew, the dear, dear girl who had set him on its path.

'If you ask me,' said Matron, as she and her husband were packing her belongings ready for her departure the following day, 'we owe a lot to that little Jo Tugnutt. I don't quite know how, but she seems to have brought us good luck.'

'In her naïve, innocent way she has, yes.'

'Do you think we should give her a little present?'

'A good idea. She shall have a year's subscription to *Perusal*.'

Before the Second World War the post came punctually twice a day, and in the late afternoon of this next to last day of term Trubbs Minor found his copy of *Yo-Yo News* waiting for him in the hall.

He glanced through it, and then one section caught his attention.

Quarterly Prize.

This quarter's prize goes to pal G. Trubbs, of St Chauvin's School, Dorset, for a really beezer idea.

He thinks folks may be getting tired of the ordinary circular Yo-Yo.

He thinks a new model should be made in the shape of a pig that squeals 'God Save the King'!

We have to admit that this stumped us for a while, chums. How do you make a pig-shaped Yo-Yo run properly on its cord?

Look at the diagram and you'll see how we solved it.

It's an ordinary Yo-Yo with the two halves of the pig fastened to an extended axle-rod.

Neat, isn't it? Look out for this bonzer new shape in the shops.

Pal Trubbs gets a posh book.

'Gosh,' said Trubbs, thrilled. His name in print, and as the winner of an award, too!

He must show this to Tugnutt at once!

I bet she'll be jolly sorry she agreed not to marry me now, he said to himself. But of course marriage to anyone, ever, was now out of the question. He was destined for higher things.

Josephine, feeling a great need for relaxation, told Porson about the new meeting place, and early that evening, using a torch in brief flashes, they slipped into the fields and picked their way along the backs of the garages to the corner overhung by a tree. She felt exceptionally tender towards him this evening and held him close and pressed her cheek to his. He was delighted, poor boy, because for her to demonstrate affection rather than just submit to it was what he craved.

But there was no help for them. The atmosphere here, although they were strictly outside the school boundary, was very strong. It was ten times more oppressive than thundery weather. It was over-powering. They broke their embrace and stared at each other apprehensively.

They heard feet lolloping on the grass, and heavy breathing from a deep throat. They heard snarling like the gargling of the letter 'r'. The creature was so close that they could almost feel the heat of its breath.

And yet they could not see it.

Josephine, remembering their last encounter, whispered, 'Tell it to go away.'

Porson was shaking. The supernatural scares unbelievers with especial force. But never did he lose his prefectorial command. He steeled himself and called out sternly, as before: 'Get away! Get away at once!'

The snarling ceased; the panting ceased; and there was a patter of retreating paws.

'Phew! It did, too,' said Porson.

Whereupon Josephine, who was given to flashes of revelation, rather as those people must be who are suddenly converted to religion, realized that she believed in the Dorset Wolf. This, in 1932, required rare sensibility. We people of today, aware of the mutations caused by nuclear fall-out or the misuse of drugs, and open-minded about ouija boards, witchcraft, astrology, etc., know how near to the world of daylight is the world of nightmare; but the people of 1932 were more rationalistic than we, and simpler minded. They were fond of explaining the inexplicable in the terms of psychology. 'All in the mind' was their newly coined, popular phrase. They had not yet realized what a bottomless pit the mind actually is.

And she felt a flood of compassion for this creature, who was still so much a schoolboy that the head prefect's command could turn it away. It was crying in the wilderness, and it needed help. It was her last 'case', and certainly the most in need.

'Let's go in,' she said.

'It's all right now.'

'But I'm not. Let's go in.'

'Let's go behind the library.'

'No, I'm sorry, Andrew. I want to be alone.'

'Oh, all right,' he said dejectedly. But when he walked across the Lower Quad he found that his knees would hardly hold him up and he was glad of the respite, after all.

Josephine needed no respite. She had told the truth: she just wanted to be alone. As soon as Porson had gone she slipped from her room again, and through the garage, and into the field.

'Woolf?' she called softly. 'Woolf, Woolf?'

Woolf was cagey. Once again the lolloping feet, the panting breath and the uvular snarl, but no appearance. He lurked in shadows, ready to dash if she moved.

This was very trying, but Josephine was patient. The lad was no doubt embarrassed by his appearance. It must be most distressing for him, one of the elite of England's youth, to have to run about on all fours with his tongue hanging out.

Nevertheless this game of hide-and-seek would get them nowhere.

'Woolf, I'm a friend.'

A snarl. No doubt he had acquired a wolf's outlook on the value of human friendship.

'I want to help you. Please show yourself.'

'Hurr, hurr, hurr,' came the heavy breathing.

'Don't you want me to help you?'

Silence.

'Woolf,' began Josephine again, trying a new tack, 'Mr Victor – '

At this, Woolf uttered a long, dismal wolf-howl. It was an immature sort of howl, a puppyish whine, and most affecting. No one in the school heard it except Mr Victor himself, who was nearest to this place. It shattered his nerves as a note will shatter a glass, and he began gibbering and wrestling with wires as if fighting his way out of a nest of snakes.

Josephine began talking rapidly and urgently. 'Woolf, Mr Victor got you into this state. Mr Victor doesn't know what he's doing, but he's got hold of some sort of magic power and he's doing awful damage with it. He's made you like this and you've got to face him with it. You're not going to get anywhere just running about Dorset being a legend.'

Woolf set up a prolonged and doubtful whimpering.

'Perhaps seeing you will jog his memory.'

Fearful and undecided whimpering.

'I'll go with you. Let's face him together.'

Low, troubled whining.

'Look,' said Josephine desperately, 'as a St Chauvin's man you can't let someone else get into a scrape. It's not cricket, Woolf. I know for certain that at this very moment Mr Victor is trying to make another monst – ' She checked herself and amended this ' – to create some other poor thing who would be much better left alone. Even if you're content to remain as you are it's up to you to protest. Play up,' she added, with inspiration, 'play up and play the game.'

So long a silence followed that she began to think that

Woolf had slunk away. Then there was a rustling in the bushes, and he came out and stood before her.

He was surprisingly small and slender, half-way between wolf and cub, whippet-sized. Only his noisy feet had given the impression of his being full grown. They were enormous.

So this was the Dorset Wolf. He was as endearing as a waif on the cinema screen.

'You're a good boy,' said Josephine. 'Now come with me.'

He trotted at her side, looking up at her steadily and trustingly, as a former wolf once looked at St Francis.

Fearless, tense with nerves, slipped round the wall of the Lower Quad and approached the garage from the far end. He was half-way there when the door of the garage nearest the Old Building inched open and Tugnutt emerged, followed by a lean, grey, sinister figure.

'God!' said Fearless, going white.

She *was* in league with Victor, then.

That crack about 'You might find I had teeth'!

The two slipped into the building through the disused scullery door. Ah yes, she knew, she knew the way. She must be preparing an ambush.

He turned, raced back to his dormitory, and began flinging things into a suitcase.

French Marie plodded reluctantly up the path through the fields. Her stomach was fluttering. She would be glad to be rid of this business. She could have outstared Medusa, but fear of the uncanny was her weakness, and to climb those dark stairs in that laden atmosphere was a prospect she dreaded.

Mr Mundy set out for Josephine's room to acquaint her

of his generosity. At exactly the same time, Mr Cropper and Trubbs Minor converged on the Old Building, entering it together, to find themselves following him down the corridor. They fell into line, Trubbs behind the two adults. All three were naturally vexed at finding themselves in company. All three wanted to be last.

'After you, old man,' said Mr Mundy to Mr Cropper.

'No, after you, sir, I insist.'

'Perhaps this lad should go first. You won't be long, will you, son?'

'After you, sir, *please*,' said Trubbs coldly. This familiar person should remember he was addressing the Captain of Yo-Yo.

'Will you be long?' said Mr Mundy to Mr Cropper. A subscription to *Perusal* should be given ceremonially, with no interlopers queueing outside.

'I may well be some time,' said Mr Cropper politely but firmly. The poor man had been hoping, with great daring, to ask Josephine to take a cup of tea with him.

This dialogue, civil but edged with acrimony, began as Josephine entered the disused scullery. She heard it and was perturbed. Woolf was not ready for a public appearance yet. She looked at his eager and adoring face.

'Wait,' she whispered. 'I'll get rid of them.'

She crept from the scullery and, in the shadows behind the stairs, managed to reach them unnoticed, and then made loud, brisk noises of descending them.

'Why, good evening, sir,' she said brightly. 'Good evening, Mr Mundy. Good evening, Trubbs.'

At this moment French Marie entered the scullery.

At this same moment Mr Victor, who had been in a frenzy for some minutes, found his Ray again.

This, like the rediscovery of the Lost Chord, was probably a pure accident. But the air was affected by a peculiar spasm, not an explosion this time, almost the opposite: a release of pressure like the drawing of a cork. The air became astonishingly light and fresh. It was as if dawn had come at midnight in a single blink. The four people below stared at one another in wonder.

Before they could speak, the light fresh air was rent by scream after shattering scream and from the shadows came rushing French Marie, her black hair flying loose, her eyes rolling in her head. She fell at their feet in a faint.

Josephine gave her one glance, jumped over her body, and rushed back to the scullery. Woolf was no longer there. She ran out into the Lower Quad. It was filling with boys and masters, aroused by the screams, and advancing like the Light Brigade. She sprang back, dithered for a moment, and then dashed upstairs to Mr Victor. She found him standing on his head in a waste-paper basket. She extricated him solicitously, and assisted him to a sitting position. He was wild-eyed and covered with dust.

'What went wrong this time? What went *wrong*?'

'Sh-sh. It's all right. It's gone right, sir.'

'No – no – '

'Really. Really it has.'

But he was inconsolable. He stared unseeingly into her face. 'It's God,' he cried. 'He's jealous of me.'

'I'll bring you a nice cup of tea,' said Josephine.

She went downstairs to find that the masters and the senior boys had fallen to with the efficiency of a fire brigade and had carried the swooning woman into the san, where Matron was attending to her. Soon she came to, babbling feverishly. Her babble was further confused by bursts of French, but they were able to make out, roughly, that she had been accosted by a wolf, which had kept its form for a mere second and then turned into a boy in school uniform. They were coldly

150

unsympathetic. They thought her hysteria frightfully bad form. And then the Dorset Wolf was a St Chauvin's legend – almost a tradition – and they much resented its being discussed by this unspeakable outsider, a foreigner, and a woman at that. Their coldness enraged her further. She cursed them in language that would have been unprintable in 1932 and would not grace these pages either. In between curses she bawled that she ought never to have come in on this crazy scheme in the first place, and it served her right for playing with a lot of kids.

This raised some eyebrows, but of course one does not bandy words with women of a certain type. They called the police, and charged her with trespassing.

Josephine retreated from this graceless scene and went back to her room, which she found occupied by a young boy with eyes of a peculiarly pale brown.

Hearing French Marie's screams, Woolf had run out into the Lower Quad to see the whole school beginning to pour into it. The astute youth had waited aside until the crowd reached him, and then joined it as his most effective hiding place. He had charged down the corridor with the others and then, adept at concealing himself, had taken refuge in Josephine's room.

'Oh, is this room yours?' he said in an aristocratic voice. 'I hope you don't think it's awful cheek, but I thought I'd better keep out of the way for a bit. I really should report to Matron, but she seems to be busy just now.'

'You're welcome,' said Josephine. 'May I introduce myself? Josephine Tugnutt.'

'Miss Tugnutt, you're the only person who has ever treated me as a human being.'

'You can't blame the others altogether.'

'You've been awfully decent.'

'Don't mention it,' said Josephine, and put the kettle on.

She found Mr Victor, however, in a state past the healing power of a nice cup of tea. She had difficulty in getting him attention. He was eventually carted back to the Cottage Hospital, throwing the Irish Sister and her staff into a state of near mutiny.

'He'll never get away with it,' said Porson.

'It seems to me he's done so,' said Josephine.

Fearless had quietly walked out of St Chauvin's with his suitcase some little while before the commotion and had not been seen since.

'My uncle', said Josephine, 'says that it is part of the great code of the school that a St Chauvin's man cannot do a dishonourable thing.'

'He should know,' said Porson, with a sigh.

Strangely, he was the only one who cared. The rest of the school was experiencing an extraordinary wave of euphoria. It would have engulfed Porson himself, but he would not let it. Discipline must be kept.

'So the matter will be quietly dropped.'

'Andrew, darling, look on the bright side. The dating agency scheme is off, the honour of the school is saved, and you're coming to spend Christmas with my family.'

'Mm,' said Porson, much consoled.

Then Josephine, perversely, could not help saying, 'I wonder what will become of Fearless?'

'Or any of us,' she added, and felt sad.

Now that over half a century has gone by that need not be a secret.

Woolf, the next term, slipped back quietly into his class. He was a dignified boy whose personality discouraged inquisitiveness. It is pleasing to report that he did well in his studies, especially in natural history.

Trubbs Minor's character was so transformed by his success at school that he entered the wider world with all the self-assurance that only a great public school can give. Eventually he became an important official in the Inland Water Transport Board, and made a name for himself as a spin bowler in their cricket club.

Mr Victor spent much of the rest of his life in mental homes, from where, like some of our best poets, he issued periodic evidences of his genius. He is included among the pioneers of nuclear fission.

Mr and Mrs Mundy went on living together, separating from time to time, until he was posted overseas during the war when she all but pined away for him. It is not known how they arranged things after that.

Fearless, having ceased very hurriedly to be of the Fifth, was immediately employed as a trainee publicity manager by Cardew's father, who was impressed with his gift for organization. Soon afterwards he started up in the same line of business on his own, and became owner of a number of clubs. He was knighted in 1961. The school acknowledged this honour by creating a Sir Frank Fearless Prize for Utter Decency.

Mr Cropper lived into his late nineties, unknown as Mr Cropper but world famous as Angela Greaves, Penelope Waynefleet, Charmian Moone, Phillida Grayle and Andromeda Starr. The work of all these authors is marked by a flair for wildness of emotion exceeding that even of the late, great Elsie M. Dingle. He had a mansion built on the Isle of Wight, which he left in his will, together with the rest of his fortune, to Josephine.

And Josephine?

She did, of course, become a psychiatrist; there was no other possible career. The surprise is that she really did marry Porson, but not until she was forty-two years old. By then she had rejected many offers of marriage. Happening to open a new bank account, she found Porson managing the bank with all his old patient assiduity. Learning that he was still single, she decided that she was tired of being Miss Tugnutt and married him within a few weeks.

And they lived happily (it is charitable to assume) ever after.

JOSEPHINE

by the same author

JONAH'S MIRROR
AN ASH-BLONDE WITCH
FULL MOON
SELKIE
ISABEL'S DOUBLE
WHAT BECKONING GHOST
YOUNG MAN OF MORNING

for younger children
THE HALLOWE'EN CAT
GABRIELLE